CHARIOTS TO CHINA

GOD'S TOUGH GUYS

Stephen, *the First Martyr*
Samuel Kirkland, *Misionary to the Senecas*
St. Vincent de Paul, *Priest and Pirate Captive*
Eric Liddell, *Olympic Star*

GOD'S TOUGH GUYS

CHARIOTS TO CHINA

A Story of Eric Liddell

DENISE WILLIAMSON

Illustrated by JIM HSIEH

Wolgemuth & Hyatt, Publishers, Inc.
Brentwood, Tennessee

Wolgemuth & Hyatt, Publishers, Inc.
1749 Mallory Lane, Brentwood, Tennessee 37027

Book Development by March Media, Inc., Brentwood, Tennessee

First Edition July 1991

PRINTED IN THE UNITED STATES OF AMERICA

Library of Congress Cataloging-in-Publication Data

Williamson, Denise J., 1954–
    Chariots to China : a story of Eric Liddell / Denise Williamson.--1st ed.
      p.   cm. — (God's tough guys)
    Summary: Describes how former Olympic star Eric Liddell helped a young Chinese boy discover courage and the love of God during a Japanese invasion of his town.
    ISBN 1-56121-058-7
    1. Liddell, Eric, 1902-1945—Juvenile literature.
  2. Missionaries—China—Biography—Juvenile literature.
  3. Missionaries—Scotland—Biography—Juvenile literature.
  4. Runners (Sports)—Scotland—Biography—Juvenile literature.
  [1. Liddell, Eric, 1902-1945. 2. Missionaries. 3. China.]
I. Title. II. Series: Williamson, Denise J., 1954–   God's tough guys.
BV3427.W55   1991
266'.52'092—dc20
[B]   91-3901
                                       CIP
                                       AC

For the
Overseas Missionary Fellowship
workers at Lammermuir House
who let me look through
the window of memory
into China's past

I consider my life worth nothing to me, if only I may finish the race and complete the task the Lord Jesus has given me—the task of testifying to the gospel of God's grace.

—*Acts 20:24*

CONTENTS

1   Night Raid   9

2   All One Home   23

3   In Enemy Territory   41

4   The Temple of Despair   57

5   A Fear of Things to Come   75

6   Separate Ways   89

7   The Peacemakers   99

8   Happy New Year 113

    Historical Note 125

1

NIGHT RAID

The year's last moon hung like a curved strip of silver above the great dry plain of China. Below it, in one of the hundred courtyards filling up the village of Nan Kung, young Wong Kwei Er braved the darkness to feed his uncle's mule.

Kicking open the high, unlatched garden gate with one cloth shoe, Kwei Er entered the dark winter plot. He called softly, "P'ing Tan, come for your supper."

Though Kwei Er did not see the mule, who was as black as the night itself, he soon felt P'ing Tan's warm breath against his chilly hands. He dropped the wheat-stalks he had carried in and stood under the dim light of heaven listening to P'ing eat.

The cold breeze played with strands of Kwei Er's hair. The sharpness of the air reminded him of other winter nights. Suddenly he was digging his fingers into P'ing's short, coarse mane as the terrors of last winter rushed in on him again. More chilling than the wind, his thoughts set him trembling.

He remembered Father forced from his boat on the

Grand Canal to join the Chinese army. Then wild-faced Japanese had spilled into their tiny waterside town, torturing, shooting, burning anyone who blocked their way. In the midst of the horror, Mother's steel grip had numbed his arm. With his three sisters crying, they had raced through fiery streets as their village burned.

Cold and hunger had chased them like twin tigers for thirty days after the night of their escape. There had been no strength to walk farther, when they finally pulled themselves to Uncle's gate.

Kwei Er locked his jaw against the bitter past, but still the pain burned down deep within his throat.

P'ing Tan's snorting made him blink his thoughts away. "We're both out here pitying ourselves," he said with a sorry laugh. "You because of lack of food. And me . . . ?" He stopped his mind from wandering again by grabbing the mule's rope halter. "Come on. We both have much to be grateful for," he said, leading P'ing to the wooden shed Uncle had built for him against the thick mud wall. The bulky two-wheeled cart that P'ing pulled by day was already there.

Now that his eyes had adjusted to the darkness, Kwei Er easily led the mule into his slender stall. "Mother's eldest brother is most kind to both of us," Kwei Er said aloud when his fingers found the iron ring bolted to the stall boards. "This year I have become like a son to him, since he has no boy-children of his own." He looped the rope dangling from P'ing's halter through the ring. "And you should be grateful, too. He built you this shelter to keep you out of sight each night."

P'ing Tan tossed his head in protest as Kwei Er tied the quick, tight knot Uncle had taught him. "It's for your own good," Kwei Er chided. "Nationalist soldiers and Communist bandits both roam the countryside looking for supplies. And we don't want them finding you!"

A shiver went up Kwei Er's backbone.

P'ing stamped impatiently.

"You think only of your unhappiness!" he huffed. "This is the last night of the dying year, and between the war with Japan and all the raiders near here not one family in Nan Kung has enough money to celebrate the New Year with gifts or food!" P'ing pressed his nose into the corner, and Kwei Er quit his one-mouthed conversation. *It was useless to waste words on a mule!*

He left the garden, pulling closed the high, bulky gate behind him. As he did, something moved along the top of his neighbor's mud wall. Fear brushed Kwei Er's back. He crouched and squinted into the night. But the jagged rooftops were as still as carvings now. With shaky hands he stood and locked the gate. Anxiety snapped at his heels as he scurried around to the front of Uncle's house.

If Ma Chuang Fu's paper window had not been black with sleep, Kwei Er might have gone inside to speak to Uncle. Instead he went to his own one-room house, pressed against the courtyard's western wall. Through the doorway Kwei Er saw that a wick still glowed in Mother's little bowl of oil. He paused, listening for danger and watching the flickering light paint dim yellow squares on the hard clay at his feet. Hearing nothing unusual, he finally went inside.

Though his mother did not look up from her cotton weaving on the loom, Kwei Er felt the happy security of home. He sat down on his hard cold cot. Beside him, his three small sisters lay giggling together in another, slightly larger bed. He reached to pull the curtain that separated their sleeping quarters. Just then four quick knocks throbbed against the courtyard gate.

Kwei Er jumped. He hurried to the doorway. Mother and his sisters peered out, too. "Who would risk meeting bandits to come here after dark?" Mother whispered.

"It is a goblin! Or that New Year's eve devil *Pi-hutze* who steals from the poor!" First Younger Sister cried, taking hold of her high tight pigtails.

"Hush!" Mother scolded as Baby Sister toddled into her arms. "Uncle is teaching us not to believe such things." His other sisters quivered against Kwei Er's waist as two more knocks sounded on the gate.

Uncle came outside with a candle in his hand. He was followed closely by Aunt, her hair hanging down. "See who has come!" Uncle called to him.

On trembling legs, Kwei Er went to put his ear against the rough wood. "Who is here?" he demanded as firmly as he could.

"Yao Feng's son. I come before the old year dies to pay my father's debt."

Kwei Er looked at Uncle. Though his beardless face was tight with concern, Ma Chuang Fu nodded for Kwei Er to open the gate.

A lanky boy several years older than Kwei Er dashed in, as though he feared the night as much as Kwei Er did. His short jacket, buttoned close to his throat, made him even more the still-water reflection of his father Yao Feng, who sold salt in the streets.

The boy bowed to Ma Chuang Fu. "My father

wishes to pay the debt he owes you. By doing this, we hope for better luck in the coming year."

Though Uncle no longer held to such beliefs, he took the large basket vibrating in the boy's hands. Opening it, he pulled out a scrawny hen. The chicken's wings flapped as she hung upside-down from the cord around her feet.

Kwei Er's mouth watered. All year, meat had been rarer than silver in Hopei province. Now Yao Feng was paying them with a hen! *There will be feasting this New Year's Day after all!* Kwei Er thought excitedly.

Then he saw Uncle frown as he put a hand to his short gray hair. "Are you sure your father wants the bird brought here?"

"Oh, yes," Yao's son answered.

Uncle surveyed him for a moment. "I'm surprised he sent you out so late. Hasn't he heard that starving soldiers have been raiding nearby towns? Doesn't he think it is unsafe for you to walk even the hundred steps from your gate to ours?"

The boy looked down. "Y-yes, he knows these things. But debts must be paid tonight if we are to expect a better future."

The women and girls crowded in for a look at the bird. "We will cook her this very night!" Aunt exclaimed.

"Don't cook her! Feed her! Keep her for eggs!" Yao's son insisted. Then looking nervously at Uncle he calmed himself. "You see, she is the best laying hen I ever raised. And if you let her peck around your mule's feet, I am sure she will survive and reward you with many eggs."

Uncle shook his head. "I am an honest man. I cannot take a valuable hen for the small debt your father owes."

"But you must!" the boy cried. "Another debt collector camps on Father's doorstep waiting to have her for his wife's cooking pot. I had to climb over the back walls to get here before Father gives her to him."

Uncle eyed him sharply. "I thought you said your father wanted me to have this hen."

"Oh! Yes! My father!" the boy gulped.

"Your parents don't even know you are here now, do they?" Uncle guessed.

The boy looked away. "What does it matter? I am paying Father's debt to you. You will have eggs if you feed this bird, and my hen will be safe. Is that not enough?"

"No," Uncle answered. "I do not want Yao Feng to think that I approve of sons who do business behind their fathers' backs—because I do not!"

The boy seemed amazed. "From what everyone says, I thought you would take my bird without question."

Uncle squinted. "And just what does everyone say?"

Yao's son dragged a a toe through the dirt. "Th-that you are like the foreigners who care nothing about our ideas or the worship of our gods."

Uncle grew tense. "But I do worship! I now believe in one true God, who wrote ten Great Commandments for us to live by. And the fifth one of them is this—You shall honor your father and mother, so that you may live long in the land."

Sudden fear caused the boy to stare in silence. "I—I have never heard you speak of this before," he stammered. "Forgive me. I should have never come."

Uncle sighed thoughtfully. "Listen. It would be very difficult for me to keep a hen and my mule. Still, if Kwei Er's sisters would let her loose in the garden while we are traveling each day, I think she could eat enough to keep on laying eggs."

Kwei Er felt his own hopes rising as Yao's son looked at Uncle with brighter eyes.

Uncle showed a slight smile. "We could share the eggs—half for your family and half for mine."

Yao's son clasped his hands. "Oh, seeing the extra food we could have, I'm sure Father will agree! I will climb back over the walls to ask him right away."

"No, you will go by the street and I will go with you," Uncle said. "Then I will know you are safe and I will see for myself what your father says." Uncle picked up the bird to carry her home.

Yao's son hesitated in the courtyard. "I do not wish to continue asking favors, Lao Ma," the boy said addressing Uncle with the title of respect, "but could we leave the hen here so that the man in our doorway does not see her?"

"All right." Uncle put the hen back into her basket. "I will come back for her myself, if your father does not want the bird kept here." He looked to Kwei Er. "Bar the gate behind us. I will be back before this hour ends."

As Uncle and Yao's son headed down the street, Kwei Er put the timber beam into its wooden brackets to secure the courtyard. He turned to find his six-year-old sister begging Aunt to free the bird. "Can't we untie

15

her?" First Younger Sister pleaded as she took the lid off the basket.

Aunt shrugged, so Mother slipped the knot in the cord. Immediately the bird sat up, hopped out, and raced around the courtyard. The three little girls screamed with delight. They chased the hen against each wall, then into their house, and up onto their bed.

"Can she sleep with us?" four-year-old Second Younger Sister begged.

"No!" Mother shouted as she rushed in behind them. "Kwei Er, put this bird in the garden." It took several wild turns around the small house before Kwei Er had the skinny chicken under his arm. He held her tightly until he reached the garden gate. As he touched the latch, a small avalanche of broken tile rattled down his neighbor's roof.

Startled, Kwei Er looked up. Two men flattened themselves against the rooftop. They had rifles strapped to their backs. Kwei Er ducked, keeping his eyes only high enough to watch what they were doing. The men made their way to the ridge of the roof. They stood and pointed their guns into the street.

Squeezing the hen to his throbbing chest, Kwei Er sprinted back between the two homes in Uncle's courtyard. "Aunt! Mother!" he gulped breathless. "Men! Armed men on the neighbor's roof!"

Shots rang out.

"Bandits!" Aunt screamed. "We must hide, in case they are strong enough to climb our walls!"

The next moment the steel blade of a bayonet shot in between the two sections of their courtyard gate. Two hands appeared on the top of the wall. "The bandits are

climbing in!'' Mother cried as tense Chinese voices sounded outside. The girls' eyes were wide with terror.

Kwei Er threw down the hen. He grabbed the children's hands. "Quick! To the garden!"

They were at the back gate when Second Younger Sister broke away. "We cannot let the bandits get our hen!"

Kwei Er raced after her. He caught her just as she scooped the chicken up into her arms. "A moment more, and it will be too late!" he cried, herding the children, Mother, and Aunt into the black garden plot.

"Go into P'ing's stall and be quiet!" he ordered, instantly deciding what to do. "But First Sister, stay! I need your help."

Kwei Er kept her by the hand while he pushed the gate shut. In the darkness he hoisted the six-year-old up onto his shoulders. "I will hold you by your ankles," he panted. "You must reach over the garden gate and latch it, so that it looks like no one has come through tonight."

He heard her frightened sobs as he stood on tiptoes, stretched his arms to the top of the gate, and braced his head against the wood. "I can't reach it! I can't reach it!" she cried, hanging down over the other side.

"You can!" he called. "You must!"

Just as the triumphant shouts of raiders exploded into the courtyard beyond them, the task was done. Kwei Er pulled his sister down into his arms and raced into the stall.

P'ing shifted nervously with so many visitors packed around his belly. Silently Kwei Er made his way to the mule's unseen face. He put his lips against P'ing's cheek. "Uncle named you 'Mild Peace' for such a time as this," Kwei Er whispered to him. "You must live up to your name."

Then with words even more breathless than these, Kwei Er called out to the Creator of Heaven and Earth. *Give us silence,* he pleaded, *and strength of heart.*

Shouts, evil words, and gunfire broke the air around them as they huddled against the mule. Their legs were numbed right up to their waists before Nan Kung grew quiet once again.

"It is still not safe to move," Aunt warned quietly. "The bandits could make a second sweep through town."

Second Younger Sister sniffled. "This hen is as heavy as a sack of gold," she moaned. "I cannot hold her anymore."

"Give her to me," Kwei Er whispered. "I thought you were foolish to stop for her. But now I am glad she is saved."

He put First Younger Sister down as feathers touched his hand. P'ing jerked when the hen passed by his nose.

"Quiet, you!" Kwei Er said to the mule. But P'ing tossed his head again.

"I am afraid of this big old creature!" Second Younger Sister pulled at Kwei Er's waist while P'ing moved restlessly from side to side.

"The chicken makes the mule act this way!" Aunt cried suddenly. "Quick! Get out before . . . !" But the rest of her words were drowned by P'ing Tan's sudden, awful braying.

Kwei Er tossed the hen out through the tiny shed

window. The women and children scattered, moments before P'ing Tan started kicking the walls.

"Quiet, you!" Kwei Er yelled, risking his safety to stay inside. "You'll call every bandit in on us for sure!" But P'ing Tan was an entirely different creature now. Swinging his great curved nose, he knocked Kwei Er's head against the wall.

"Get out!" Mother cried outside the window. "You'll be killed!"

Kwei Er hoisted himself through the paneless opening while P'ing ranted on with brays and kicks.

Suddenly they were trapped in the ivory-colored light of a lantern swinging through the garden gate.

"We are lost because of a stupid hen!" Kwei Er moaned in angry terror. But when he looked beyond the light, he saw the face of his uncle Ma Chuang Fu.

"You are all safe? And even P'ing Tan is not stolen?" Uncle cried joyfully, seeing them and hearing his mule's wild voice.

"It is because Kwei Er had me lock the gate!" First Young Sister blurted out proudly.

Uncle's eyes warmed to Kwei Er. "It is a miracle from heaven!" Then he rushed to the window of P'ing Tan's stall.

"It was the chicken," Kwei Er said running up beside him. "Second Younger Sister brought her in when we were hiding here."

Uncle gave him an impatient glance. "You have been working with me for almost a year, Nephew. Don't you know P'ing Tan loses all sense when chickens cross his path?"

"Not until this moment, Uncle," Kwei Er replied

shyly. "Since I have been on the roads with you, the countryside has been too poor for hens."

He saw Uncle shake his head. "Well, now, Kwei Er, remember you have been warned. And be thankful that this knowledge came to you without injury." Holding his light higher he pointed to his own lips. "P'ing first let me know his fears the day I bought him. A rooster hopped the wall beside us. P'ing tried killing it with a kick. The old bird was fast enough to live—but I lost three of my front teeth!"

Despite their troubles, Uncle chuckled softly. "Of course, I have forgiven him. But the hole in my mouth reminds me to be on guard for chickens."

"This is a good thing to know." In the darkness Kwei Er smiled.

"You laugh with bandits right outside?" Aunt gasped.

Uncle shook his head. "They are gone. They took as much as they could carry." He handed the lantern to Kwei Er, calmed P'ing Tan with a word through the window, and finally risked going into the stall. Then to Kwei Er's surprise, Uncle backed the mule out into the night.

"Get the cart," he said. "We must get to Siao-chang."

"Through a thousand dangers!" Aunt protested.

But Uncle was already hauling out the leather harness. He slipped the padded collar over P'ing's head. "I was near Yao Feng's house when bandits broke in. He refused to unlock his salt supply. The raiders tied him to the rafters and sliced his hands and wrists. I hid until I could get in. I have bandaged his arms to slow the bleeding. But only Li Mu Shi can find a Western doctor skilled enough to treat such wounds."

A pit formed in Kwei Er's stomach. He handed the lantern to Mother. In the darkness, he felt his way to the cart. Backing into the shed, he wrapped his arms around the two wooden cart shafts. He grit his teeth and pulled with all his strength. Though Uncle had been sacrificing food from his own bowl to make Kwei Er strong, his limbs were still too small for the size of the task. Fear, mixed with his straining, weakened his knees even more.

With worried eyes his mother and sisters watched him work. Finally Aunt helped him move the cart into place. "You cannot take your sister's only son into such danger!" she said to Uncle. "Carters are killed and their mules are hauled away on nights like this one."

But Uncle pulled the straps tight to complete the harness. "I know ten different routes to Siaochang. But I need Kwei Er's good hearing and sharp eyes to choose the safest way." Calmly he took the rope hanging loose from P'ing Tan's halter. "Get up. Get up."

Kwei Er's belly was in a hundred knots. Still he put his hands to the back of the cart and guided it cleanly through the gate behind Uncle and the mule. At the courtyard entryway, Uncle paused. "I have checked the bar," he said to Aunt. "It is still strong. Lock the gate after we leave. Even if trouble does not find us, we will have an hour's walk each way. At the earliest, you can expect us to return at dawn."

2

ALL ONE
HOME

Except for the creaking of P'ing Tan's cart, Nan Kung was as silent as a coffin. When they reached Yao Feng's house, Kwei Er saw that the gate had been smashed. Broken red candles and paper money lay scattered near an overturned table in the courtyard. Uncle led P'ing around what remained of the New Year's offering. He tied the mule to the battered doorframe while Yao's son greeted them anxiously.

"A Western doctor can heal your father. I am sure of it," Uncle said to comfort him. But the tall boy only squeezed his hand against his stomach and took them inside.

Yao Feng lay on the floor, his wife kneeling beside him.

"As I promised, I have brought my cart to take you to the Jesus Mission at Siaochang," Uncle said, bending down beside his injured friend.

"And . . . as I told you before . . . I do not wish to go," Yao struggled. He studied the bulky bandages that hid his wrists and hands.

"You will find Li Mu Shi very kind when you meet him—" Uncle began hopefully.

"I do not like any foreign devil!" The man grimmaced with pain. "And especially this Liddell man who calls himself by a Chinese name!"

"No, it is his Chinese friends who give Eric Liddell the name *Li Mu Shi*," Uncle explained. "It is what we also called his father, who worked in Siaochang when I was growing up there."

"All foreign devils deserve mistrust!" Yao growled.

"Not Li Mu Shi. He belongs to China, even as our own sons do," Uncle reasoned. "He was born here, and that is why he chooses to be here now. Oh yes, he has the pale eyes and hair of a foreigner, but as soon as he speaks, you will see—he has a Chinese mind and heart."

The salt seller's eyes were dark like polished wood. "If this were true, he would not want you to move me from my home." Yao turned his face to the rafters. "What right do you have to interfere? Misfortune has come to my house tonight. Perhaps fate says this is my time to die."

"You are my friend, in both sweet and bitter times," Uncle said.

When Yao Feng did not respond, Uncle glanced back at Kwei Er and Yao's son who stood behind him. Then he bent close to the man. "I have never said this to anyone outside my family, but I believe God can speak to me through his Spirit. There is an urgency inside my heart. I must take you with me. You see, this may be the silent voice of God I hear."

At this Yao Feng moaned and turned his head to Uncle. "Do not believe it, Ma Chuang Fu. How can you be fooled to think of only one God, as the missionaries do? How can the same unseen power that was great enough to light the sun also be small enough to hear a man breathe?"

"Through Jesus, God's son, who walked on the earth. His Spirit desires to live inside us," Uncle answered quickly and with words so soft Kwei Er could barely understand them. "You have seen the poster that hangs in my house. The man dying on the plank of wood is God himself. He suffered to show us love and to win us back to himself from all idols and other ways of living."

Yao smiled glumly as he looked away. "You may be the best storyteller in all of Hopei province . . . but you will never have me believing such a tale." He closed his eyes. "I trust what our fathers taught us: When evil traps one man, it is dangerous for another to pull him from the pit. Go away, my friend. Do not risk bringing danger to your family or yourself by helping me."

"I am taking you to Siaochang." There was sudden strength in Uncle's voice. "We will talk about beliefs again when you are well."

"I will not accept foreign teaching just so Western doctors can save my life!" Yao panted as Uncle raised him to his feet.

"No one will ask you to," Uncle promised.

"I will always honor the household gods and never worship yours who bleeds from his hands and feet."

"I ask nothing of you. Just help me get you to the cart." Uncle supported the weak man's weight.

Outside Kwei Er grabbed P'ing Tan's halter. He steadied the mule while Uncle and Yao's son lifted the salt seller into the cart. Uncle turned to Yao's anxious wife. "My house has a strong gate. Take your son and stay there until we return."

"Let me come with you," she pleaded suddenly. "I can help care for my husband. Then he will not be alone."

"It is too dangerous," Uncle told her.

Yao's wife wiped her eyes. "What if my husband speaks the truth? Then you and Kwei Er are in great danger now."

Uncle seemed to ignore her worry. Yao slumped against the cartboards. Uncle spread two old quilts across the man's shoulders. "Tell P'ing to get up," he told Kwei Er.

Leading the mule in a tight circle, Kwei Er turned the cart from the ruined courtyard into the narrow street. Gunfire crackled nearby. Instantly P'ing Tan locked his knees.

"Get him to go on," Uncle said. "We will travel in the frozen fields, not on the roads."

Kwei Er swallowed his own fear in order to speak calm words to the mule. P'ing took a few steps backward, then went forward again. As they reached the village edge, Kwei Er sensed they were being watched. He looked across his shoulder. Tense, grime-streaked faces peeked out from the broken doorways. Some held out lanterns to help light P'ing's way.

"I am going to the Hospital at Siaochang," Uncle announced to all who looked at them. "Surely there are wounded men, women, and children who need a doctor. Come with us."

But fear tied the people to their doorsteps. Uncle and Kwei Er walked out through the charred village gates alone. They started across the icy fields while the fragile slice of moon balanced itself on the horizon. Without light of their own, Kwei Er let Uncle lead them, using his knowledge of the landscape and the feel of the ground underneath his feet.

Kwei Er strained his ears to listen. There was occasional gunfire and the constant creaking of the cart. Kwei Er took each step with hesitation, knowing quite well that it was easier to be heard than to hear on such a cold, clear night. The air slowly chilled him to his deepest bone as they walked on.

Suddenly in the thick darkness a match snapped into flame. Kwei Er crouched, until he recognized his own shadow flickering on a rough wall in front of them.

Uncle held the tiny light for a second more, then puffed it out. "Kwei Er, did you see the familiar gate of Siaochang just now? I want you to remember that it is by God's grace that we are here."

"Are you sure we are at Siaochang?" Yao Feng's uncertain voice came through the darkness. "How could you find your way for six li without any light?"

Uncle laughed. "Friend, I have been a carter for thirty years. If one cannot learn to travel his route blind in that amount of time, he should take the place of his mule."

Kwei Er heard Yao Feng's weak chuckle, then his voice was serious again. "What do the words above the gate mean? I did not have time to read them in the light."

Knowing that Uncle could not read even the characters of his own name, Kwei Er drew in breath. But to his surprise, Uncle answered. "The words say *'Chung Wai, I Chia,'*—Chinese and Foreigner, All One Family.

Though I have no desire to read it for myself, I have heard the signboard read countless times since my youth."

Uncle left P'ing's side to pound on the gate. "I am the hauler Ma Chuang Fu. I have an injured man."

Immediately the gates swung in for them. P'ing's hoofs clapped against the bricks as they moved inside. Light glowed from every window in the large building ahead of them. Kwei Er had never seen the hospital by night. Now he knew why Uncle called it the 'House of No Sleep'.

A dark figure from the porch came down to meet them. In the light of the small lamp the man carried, Kwei Er caught a glimpse of Li Mu Shi's tired, but friendly, face.

"Chuang Fu! Kwei Er!" the tall, pale-haired man exclaimed as he cast his light into the cart. "Have bandits raided Nan Kung, too?"

"Yes." Uncle nodded gravely. "Many could have used your help, Mu Shi, but I bring only one. He is Yao Feng, our salt seller. He needs your doctors right away."

Kwei Er watched Li Mu Shi's blue eyes, which never ceased to fascinate him. They seemed to grow even rounder as the man looked in at Yao's blood-stained bandages. "We will get you inside at once," the pastor said.

But when Li Mu Shi jumped up on the cart shaft to reach in to him, Yao Feng shouted, "Stay away."

"This is Li Mu Shi!" Uncle said. "Do you remember anything we talked about? This man is like one of us—"

Mu Shi touched Uncle's shoulder and hopped down. "Don't trouble him with all this now. I will take

your mule. Kwei Er can help you bring your friend inside."

A slight smile carved a deep valley in Mu Shi's chin as he took the rope from Kwei Er's hand. "Does this mule have a name?" he asked.

"Eh, P'ing Tan," Kwei Er answered.

"Oh, I know the meaning of those words!" Mu Shi laughed, his tongue seldom struggling with the Chinese language. "They say that even *I* should have no trouble with him!"

"Unless you have chickens!" Kwei Er agreed. Then he ran to take Yao Feng's elbow as Uncle lifted the salt seller from the cart. The man staggered between them to the hospital door. Inside the huge building, strange, sour smells filled Kwei Er's nose. A foreign woman dressed in white led them into a small room with a curtain across its doorway.

"Does she always wear the color of mourning?" Yao gasped with alarm.

Uncle shook his head. "White does not mean death or mourning to these people," he explained. "It is the color of purity here."

Yao sighed, only to grow tense again when the woman laid out needles, scissors, and a set of small knives on the table beside Kwei Er. When the doctor finally crowded in with them, the room began to twist dizzily around Kwei Er's head. His eyesight went dark while the doctor exposed the first red strips of flesh on Yao Feng's right arm.

Suddenly the woman was holding Kwei Er's shoulders. "You should not be in here," she said, walking him through the curtain. "You wait in the hall."

Kwei Er fell against the wall to stop his head from spinning. He stood there for a long time, closing his eyes each time he heard Yao Feng moan.

"Kwei Er, are you out here worrying about your father's friend?" It was Mu Shi who stopped to speak as he hurried in through the front door.

Kwei Er numbly shook his head.

"Doctor McAll is a fine physician," Mu Shi said picking some straw from his thick sweater. "Yao Feng is in two very good sets of hands right now—one of them human and one divine."

Kwei Er tried to return Mu Shi's smile, but the tension of the night had taken all his energy away.

"Have you eaten?" the pastor asked.

Kwei Er did not answer, knowing it was rude to say how a half-bowl of wheat gruel at dawn had been his only meal.

Mu Shi's eyes warmed with the silence. "Come on. I just got back from a four-day trip to Tientsin a few hours ago. Now, I suddenly realize I have not eaten anything today. How about a meal with me?"

Kwei Er, marveling at how quickly food and drink could be offered here, found the strength to follow Mu Shi into a room across the hall. Here the tall, blond man turned up the lamp that sighed from a metal post on the wall. Mu Shi watched Kwei Er as the light glowed brighter. "Haven't you seen this sort of lamp before?" he asked.

Kwei Er shaded his eyes in awe. "Not lighted."

"It is called a *ch'i deng*," Mu Shi explained. "The

unseen gas that burns is carried in through this pipe. The brilliant glow is made by two fine cloth nets that allow the gas to burn without being burned themselves."

Kwei Er nodded, though he did not completely understand what Mu Shi was telling him. His attention drifted to a second wonder in the room, a shelf filled with books. But to Kwei Er's disappointment, Li Mu Shi did not speak of these. Instead he went to the doorway. "Wait here," he said. "I will find us both some supper."

When Kwei Er was alone, he put his hand against the shelf. The books—light, dark, smooth, rough—danced under his fingertips as he moved his hand along. He stopped at the first Chinese title he touched. "*Sheng . . . Ching*—The Holy Classic," he whispered to himself.

By its title Kwei Er knew this was the Chinese Bible Li Mu Shi read from every seven days when they had church at Siaochang. He had always listened carefully to Mu Shi's readings, but because of Uncle's opinions, he never looked inside the Word of God himself. He bit his lip, daring to touch the book again. "*Sheng Ching!*" He felt the pleasure of reading aloud.

The words came back to him. "*Sheng Ching!* That is right! Can you read?"

Kwei Er spun around. Mu Shi was watching him with an admiring eye.

"You can read?" Mu Shi asked again excitedly, putting down the tray with tea and two bowls of noodles.

"Yes!" Kwei Er admitted. "My father worked hard so that I could have time off from our canalboat to attend school." He gulped, thinking he had said too much. "Ahh, but please understand, Mu Shi. I do not read now that I am a hauler in Hopei."

Mu Shi gave him a sympathetic nod as he motioned for Kwei Er to sit with him at the table. "It is your Uncle's wish that you do not read."

"You are right," Kwei Er sighed, relieved that he did not have to explain the answer he had given.

Mu Shi bowed his head. He thanked God for the day, for the food, and for his time with Kwei Er. They drank and ate in silence until their chopsticks clicked against empty bowls. "Ma Chuang Fu knows that a hauler must work hard to be strong and fast enough to earn a living by taking goods from place to place," Mu Shi said. "I suppose it would not be right for such a man to have a smooth-handed nephew who only wanted to read and be a scholar."

"Yes, that is it exactly!" Kwei Er felt he might burst with his sudden desire to share his feelings and frustration. "Besides, he wants me to have a memory like his, one that can hear words once and then repeat them exactly as they have been said. Books destroy such memory. That's what Uncle thinks."

Mu Shi smiled. "He may be right, you know."

"But I want to read!" Kwei Er said not guarding his emotions. "You read! What can be wrong with it?"

Mu Shi sighed. "There are different ways of seeing things. I have encouraged your Uncle to learn how to read. I admire his fantastic memory and the way he tells a story, but sometimes I worry that he will have to live without knowing the whole Bible—if we are forced away from China."

Kwei Er felt a sudden panic. "You! Forced away! When will that happen, Mu Shi?"

Mu Shi put a hand to his high forehead. "Not soon, I hope. But someday, perhaps, it will."

Kwei Er looked at him. The bitter taste of memories soured his tongue.

Mu Shi squeezed Kwei Er's wrist. "I am learning to trust God and love his plans more than my own. This way of faith allows us to walk without fretting or fear. When you *know* God loves you completely, you do not mind *not knowing* what tomorrow holds. For me—for you—it becomes enough just to say 'I surrender myself completely to Jesus Christ today.'"

He got up and pulled the Bible from the shelf. "Here, I can't think that your uncle will mind your reading for a short time while you wait for him."

"Really?" Kwei Er asked.

Mu Shi nodded. "I must get back to work, but I will tell him where you are and what you are doing."

Kwei Er barely heard the pastor's voice. Already the story of the great flood of Noah's time was being told again inside his head as his eyes flowed down the opened pages. He leaned close to the book, losing himself in the day when all the earth disappeared beneath the stormy waters. He read the scriptures the way another boy might stuff himself at a banquet table. Only when he was drowsy with contentment did he let his hand slip from the book. He put his weary head to the table and drifted into sleep.

"Kwei Er!!!"

The sharpness of his spoken name caused him to jump to his feet. Uncle was at the doorway. "Have you been here all these hours?" His voice was heavy with anger.

"Y-yes, Uncle." Kwei Er gasped. "Mu Shi said you might not mind if I read."

"For a short time!" Uncle reminded him. "And what of P'ing? I hope you took care of him sometime tonight!"

"Oh no!" Kwei Er said, pushing himself away from the table.

Uncle scowled. His leathery skin looked dark even in the room's unnatural light. "Li Mu Shi has a job for us to do at dawn—*if we still have a cart and a mule outside!*"

Kwei Er swallowed. "Does the work concern our salt seller?"

The harshness in Uncle's face dissolved. "No. He is doing very well, though the doctors want him to stay at Siaochang until they know that his wounds are not infected. Mu Shi has found a young Chinese man to help Yao Feng, so that he will be at ease while we are away."

"Away where?" Kwei Er asked.

Uncle led Kwei Er into the hallway as he spoke. "Up North, a few li from the carters' inn at Huo Chu."

"Why, that's almost eighty li from here!" Kwei Er exclaimed. "What business can Mu Shi have that far away? Didn't he just get back from Tientsin?"

Uncle stopped near the front door. He did not hide the trouble in his eyes. "Mu Shi came through Huo Chu this morning on his way down from the North. Someone risked telling him about a wounded soldier who lies in a temple outside the village of Pei Lin Tyu. Mu Shi desires to help the man."

"Why doesn't someone up there do it?" Kwei Er asked, already dreading the journey Uncle had in mind.

"For the same reason that no other carter will bring him here." Uncle eyed him. "The area is under Japanese control, Kwei Er. Anyone who helps or hides Chinese soldiers risks being killed."

Kwei Er held his breath. Uncle raised an eyebrow. "I trust Li Mu Shi," he said. "If he feels it is God's will to rescue this man, I will provide the cart for him." Without another word, Uncle opened the hospital door.

Kwei Er's heart stopped beating as the cold night air hit his face. *P'ing Tan was not there!*

A moment later, however, Uncle and Kwei Er caught sight of their mule standing contentedly in the south corner of the courtyard. The cart was parked nearby. Uncle raced to P'ing's side, with Kwei Er only one step behind him. "You didn't take P'ing here? Or loose him from the harness? Or feed or water him?" Uncle asked.

Kwei Er shook his head, though he saw that all these things had been done.

Uncle looked around. He sighed at the sight of five other carters dozing around a small fire. Kwei Er knew they were here behind Siaochang's strong walls to wait out the night of bandit raids. "Someone there took care of him." Uncle nodded. "It is only right that I find out who it was."

"Welcome! Ma Chuang Fu!" a long-faced, bareheaded man called as Uncle took Kwei Er over to the carters' little fire. "How glad we are to see you."

Uncle and Kwei Er sat down on the bricks that had

been warmed by the flames, which flared and died and blazed again as the men added dry brush.

"We've been watching for you all night," the carter to the left of Kwei Er said. "We hoped you would help us pass the hours with some of your wonderful stories."

"Well, it's not morning yet," the man on Uncle's right put in. "Here's a coin to start you talking, but tell us only good-humored tales, like the one you know about the man who wouldn't buy shoes in the market because he had left the measurement of his feet at home."

The dark circle of men vibrated with laughter. "Yes, weren't we all trapped by rain in Chaochow the night you told that tale?"

Uncle refused the coin. "Perhaps I will tell a story or two," he said, "but not for payment, since one of you took care of my mule tonight."

Again the men shook with laughter. "You mean you do not know what happened? Hah! That's a tale worth telling in itself. We saw you unload the injured man to-night, and as soon as you went inside, that blue-eyed man you favor came right up to us and asked us how you take care of a mule."

Uncle was silenced with shame. "It was my fault!" Kwei Er fretted. "I should have come back outside right away."

"Ahh, don't be distressed about what happened!" the man on Uncle's right slapped his knee. "He did everything we told him. Who knows, the way history moves, soon all foreigners in China may find themselves put out to work in the fields."

Kwei Er felt Uncle's uneasiness.

The man across the fire narrowed his gaze. "Ma Chuang Fu, don't care too much for this man. China's seasons of power change even as her seasons of nature do. When we were young men, we saw Siaochang come into flower. But much time has passed since then. Enough to make me think that winter will soon be here for the foreign devils who live in China."

Uncle stood suddenly, dusting off his pants. "If you feel this way, why do you work for the hospital?"

"Well, there are good fruits to be taken even from dying trees," the man on Uncle's right said. "Come now, you are here for the same reason we are. The pay for carting supplies to Siaochang is fair and good."

But the man across the fire from Uncle said, "No, I think Ma Chuang Fu hauls for Li Mu Shi because he has eaten that man's Christianity."

Uncle turned on his heel. "Kwei Er, it is time to go."

Kwei Er followed with his head bent down. When they were with P'ing Tan again, Uncle started harnessing the mule. "Why do you never speak of Christianity to anyone except those who live within your household?" Kwei Er asked timidly.

Uncle glared at him. "Do you know what it would be like to be a carter and not be trusted or liked by any of your co-workers on the roads?"

Kwei Er shook his head.

"Then don't question me. I live by the teachings of Christ. That is enough. God uses people like Li Mu Shi to *preach* the Word of God."

Kwei Er looked down. The things Li Mu Shi had shared with him at supper rested heavily on his heart.

Uncle put his face to the sky. "The feel of dawn is already in the air. We will start our journey now so that we have time to go back to Nan Kung for some supplies." Going to the gate, Uncle woke the guard. The old man protested their leaving while gunshots still disturbed the air. But Uncle insisted, and soon they faced the darkness outside Siaochang once more.

3

IN ENEMY
TERRITORY

Dawn pried off the heavy shades of night just as Kwei Er and Uncle reached the edge of Nan Kung. Nothing moved in the gray streets and no voice was heard, until Uncle called out at his own courtyard gate. Yao's son let them in. Seeing the empty cart he asked, "How is Father?"

"He will be fine." Uncle smiled. "But the doctor said he could have bled to death or lost the use of his hands if he had not come to Siaochang."

The women, hearing Uncle's voice, ran to greet them. Kwei Er's sisters bounced around his feet. "Happy New Year, Uncle! Happy Year, Brother!" Unexpectedly, P'ing Tan added his wheezing brays to their shouts.

The girls laughed. But Uncle grabbed the mule's rope with both hands, ready to hang on tightly. "Where is that chicken?" he demanded.

"In the garden," Yao's son said. "I heard what happened last night. I will catch her, so you can put your mule into his stall."

41

"That is not necessary," Uncle replied. "I have come only to say that Yao Feng is doing well and to load some feed for my mule. We are on our way to Huo Chu."

"You must travel so far on this holiday?" Aunt asked quickly.

Uncle looked at Kwei Er. "Yes. It is a trip Li Mu Shi asked us to make. We must take a wounded soldier to the hospital at Siaochang."

Mother's lips parted with worry. "Please don't take Kwei Er," First Younger Sister protested. "We want to spend New Year's Day with him."

Uncle looked into her timid eyes. "I'm afraid I have to, my pretty little flower. You wait here, and soon you will know why." Then Uncle dropped P'ing's rope, barred the gate, and went into his house.

While Uncle was gone, Mother told Kwei Er to come inside and sit down on his bed. She came in behind him, removed his shoes, and lined them with precious sheep's wool for added warmth on their long journey. Before she gave them back, she pulled a hidden coin from a crack in the wall. "In case you need it!" she said concealing the money under the lining of one shoe.

"No, you must keep your money!" Kwei Er said, seeing for the first time how much the bandits had destroyed. "Your loom is broken! Your weaving is gone!"

Mother covered her sorrow. "Yao's son promises to fix the loom today. And I still have thread. So you see everything is not lost . . . unless, something happens to you!" Suddenly she threw her arms around him and hugged him to herself as though he were a little boy. "Be very careful, my child! I have heard that the Japanese control many of the roads."

Kwei Er swallowed his own tears. Through the open doorway he saw Uncle waiting with P'ing Tan. He put on his shoes and slipped his padded vest over the jacket he was wearing. Outside, he noticed that Uncle had exchanged his work trousers and coat for a fine robe. He was loading a basket of dry beans into the cart for P'ing Tan's supper.

Then as everyone watched in amazement, Uncle climbed into the cart himself. Sitting crosslegged, he wrapped the quilts around his shoulders. "Hauler, let's be on our way!"

Kwei Er, baffled at Uncle's actions, grabbed P'ing Tan's rope. But First Younger Sister would not move out of his way. She stood on tiptoes to scowl at Uncle. "Why do you treat Brother like this?"

Uncle showed a sly, toothless smile. "Because an old hauler who takes an empty cart into enemy territory will attract much attention. But a young hauler who takes his elder on a holiday visit should get no second looks at all."

Yao's son folded his arms. "You are very clever, Lao Ma! *I Lu P'ing An!*—'All the way in Peace' as you go!"

"Get this mule up!" Uncle said with a delighted nod. "If you do well, I will pay you and that long-eared friend of yours with supper tonight."

Aunt ran to them as the cart began to move. "I have something for you," she cried.

"You made *bao tyus* for New Year's day!" Uncle said with disbelief as he reached for the white dumpling in her hand. "And it is filled with meat?"

Aunt shook her head, as Kwei Er saw Yao's mother look the other way. "What's inside has been given to you by Yao's wife," Aunt explained. "I suggest you treat this dumpling with much care. What's inside is worth more to you than ten bao tyus made anywhere else."

"Ahh, I see!" Uncle said with a slow, tender smile. "I will not let this dumpling out of my sight." He paused. "You are worried about us, aren't you? You know the trip we take might not be easy."

Water come into all the women's eyes. Not wanting to see them cry, Kwei Er turned P'ing Tan into the street.

"Where is Li Mu Shi?" Yao's son called out. "I thought he was to go with you."

Uncle looked back. "We are not traveling together, but there is an old tamarisk tree about eight li from Huo Chu. We plan to rest there and wait for one another. When we meet, we will make our final plans about how to find the wounded soldier and bring him home."

Then looking to Kwei Er, Uncle wiped all familiarity from his face. "Hurry now, Carter," he called with a laugh. "It is a four- or five-hour walk to Huo Chu, and I do not wish to be late."

"Come on! P'ing Tan!" Kwei Er shouted with pretended harshness. "We have a pushy customer today. If you don't trot fast enough for him, I'll squeeze the liver from you!"

Second Younger Sister skipped out the gate after them. *"I Lu P'ing An! I Lu P'ing An!"* The music of her voice stayed with Kwei Er until they left the streets of Nan Kung.

Outside the village, stubbled wheatfields whispered in the rising wind. Kwei Er walked a short distance on the deserted road, then he risked turning back to Uncle. "There are no coolies with their carrying poles. And no other haulers!" he said nervously. "You taught me that a silent road is a road of danger. Are you sure we should go on?"

"Very few peasants work on New Year's morning," Uncle reminded him. "Do not be afraid."

Kwei Er closed his eyes. He and P'ing both bowed into the wind. Grit stung his face and found its way into his nostrils and his teeth. As he pressed on, the words of the song Uncle sang to himself whipped into Kwei Er's ears. It was a hymn Li Mu Shi liked to sing with them whenever they traveled together.

"When we walk with the Lord,
in the light of his Word,
what a glory he sheds on our way!
While we do his good will,
He abides with us still,
and with all who will trust and obey."

Uncle's voice died each time they passed the wall of some sleepy town. It would rise again whenever they were surrounded by the silent fields. As the sun warmed in color, the morning wind died away. Grateful for the milder air, Kwei Er found himself starting to sing too. But at the sight of the next town Kwei Er's mouth went dry. A white flag with the circle of the sun pictured on it flickered above the village gate.

"The Japanese have taken this town!" Kwei Er cried, forgetting the danger of looking back at Uncle. "Look. The village flies the enemy's flag!"

"Do your work, boy! Or I'll find myself a better carter!" Uncle called.

46

Uncle's harshness warned him to keep his head, but just as he forced himself to look forward again a Chinese soldier walked up to him.

"The road is closed to all but Chinese troops who support the Japanese," he announced in flat tones.

"But I must get through," Kwei Er blurted out, not knowing what to do.

"Not now," the man said. "Wait by the wall. Perhaps later you will be allowed to travel north."

Kwei Er stole a glance at Uncle.

"Do as he says," Uncle told him quietly.

Kwei Er pulled the cart to the side of the road. Immediately P'ing Tan seemed grateful for the lack of work. He lowered his head against the sun-warmed wall and promptly went to sleep. Kwei Er, however, stood tense beside the cart. Soon the first of a long line of Chinese soldiers began moving past them. The men straggled by Kwei Er without even looking in his direction. They carried weapons, bedrolls, teapots, and umbrellas. When the troops were finally gone, Kwei Er saw Uncle looking at the sun.

"We have been here at least two hours," Uncle whispered, motioning for Kwei Er to lean near to listen. "See if the guard will let you through now."

Gathering his courage, Kwei Er pulled P'ing Tan out of his slumber. He walked beside the cart to the gate where the guard who had stopped him now stood talking with another solider. To his surprise and relief, the guard motioned him to head on down the road.

When the town was far behind him, Kwei Er urged P'ing Tan to trot, knowing they should make up the time they had lost. Soon, though, the terrain grew more difficult as they wove their way through a cluster of sandy, wind-swept hills, and Kwei Er found himself walking again. Impatient for better road, he ignored the pain pounding in his side and hurried on. Finally on a spot of high ground, he saw that good road flowed out before him over the next wide, flat portion of the plain.

Kwei Er took P'ing Tan down this last slope at a trot, grateful now that travel would be easier again. "You will beat Mu Shi there, at this rate!" Uncle laughed aloud to show Kwei Er that he was pleased with his speed. Kwei Er set his face ahead, determined to win the race against the sun which was now high in the sky.

Suddenly a soldier leaped out from the shadow of the last hill. He thrust a bayonet against Kwei Er's chest. *"Bich dong!!!"* he shouted in sharp Japanese.

Kwei Er's breath stopped as he pulled P'ing Tan's rope. While he froze in fear, his eyes caught sight of two large canvas-covered supply trucks hidden in the valley between the hills.

The first soldier held his gun to Kwei Er while a second soldier, younger and taller than the first, walked back to the cart. Silently Uncle watched the man take the soybeans they carried for P'ing Tan's supper. When the soldier prodded Uncle with the point of his pistol, he jumped from the cart clutching the dumpling in his hand. The soldier eyed the food suspiciously, until Uncle took a bite from it and quietly moved to the side of the road.

"Now that old man will walk!" The soldier beside Kwei Er laughed. "We will take your mule."

"No!" Kwei Er shouted, throwing his arm around P'ing's neck. Roughly the solider pushed him away. Then he checked P'ing's eyes and teeth. "A strong worker, this one," he said happily in rough Chinese. "Now, Boy, let's take a look at you!"

Kwei Er quaked as the soldier took hold of his chin and squeezed the muscles in his arms. "Your age!" he demanded.

"E-leven years."

"Ah, just a child!" the man said with disgust. He snapped Kwei Er's face with one of his fingers. "Another year, perhaps, and I would have put you to work, too."

He yanked the rope from Kwei Er's hand. "Unhitch your mule. I will let you keep your cart. You can shoulder the harness, if the old man must ride."

Kwei Er's eyesight blurred as he struggled to undo P'ing's leather straps. All too soon the mule was being pulled away. But seeming to sense the danger, P'ing took only a few steps before locking his hoofs to the dirt.

The soldier swore at him, but P'ing moved only his two long ears. The second soldier, coming to help, slapped P'ing Tan's hip. P'ing let out a hearty bray.

Suddenly the bayonet was pointed at Kwei Er again. "You get him to the truck!" the older soldier said.

Praying that P'ing might not move for him, Kwei Er took the rope. But the mule instantly decided to walk beside Kwei Er's familiar raised hand.

Tears of hatred welled up in Kwei Er's eyes as he came to the back of the first truck. The large canvas-roofed truckbed was filled with every kind of food grown by the poor farmers of Hopei. "Tie him to the truck!" the soldier who walked beside him ordered.

Rage made Kwei Er's fingers stiff. As he finished the knot, P'ing Tan proved himself to be a traitor by greedily eating some of the cabbages that bulged through the closest crate.

The soldier, seeing this, batted P'ing Tan's nose away. "Untie him! I want him taken behind the second truck instead." Kwei Er backed P'ing away from his source of food. He moved slowly, grateful for every extra moment he had before saying good-bye to the mule. Side by side they plodded to the rear of the second vehicle. P'ing Tan was first to raise his head. Kwei Er's face shot up a moment later, when the cackle and scratching of chickens came to his ears.

"*Crates* of chickens?" Kwei Er said to the soldier, forcing his voice to be steady.

"More than a poor carter like you would see in a dozen lifetimes!" the soldier answered with a haughty laugh.

Kwei Er drew P'ing to the truck, asking God to make the hens sounds even louder. Already P'ing was tossing his head. But the soldier saw the trouble coming and grabbed the rope above Kwei Er's own tight hands. Kwei Er let go, just before P'ing Tan reared. The soldier yelped in pain, as the rope burned his hands while it slid through his grasp. Kwei Er threw himself to the ground, pressing his face into the dust. The earth vibrated with P'ing's hoofbeats. A shot broke the air. Kwei Er raised his head in terror, then almost grinned when he saw the mule running free far out in the distance fields.

"Get up, you fool!" the younger soldier said, grabbing Kwei Er by the edge of his vest. "I know what to do with boys like you." But as his pistol came aside Kwei Er's face, the older soldier stopped his action with a few quick words in Japanese.

Kwei Er let his eyes move to see what they were waiting for. A thin line of dust curved down the hill. It was being stirred up as Li Mu Shi glided down the slope on his bicycle.

"You and the old man sit by the road. One sound, and I will finish what I started to do with you!" the younger soldier warned.

Quickly Kwei Er ran and grabbed Uncle's cold, stiff hand. "The soldier says we must sit and stay silent."

"Then sit, my brave nephew!" Uncle said, pulling him down into the dirt. "But do not stay silent. Inside, call out to the God of Heaven to help us and Li Mu Shi."

As Uncle spoke the soldiers stepped in front of Mu Shi's bicycle. The back tire skidded sideways as Mu Shi was forced to the instant halt. The soldiers spoke in Japanese to each other, and then in Chinese to Mu Shi who stood gathering his breath after his hard, fast ride. Every word exchanged between them came to Kwei Er on the breeze.

"Who are you? What is your business?" the older soldier demanded.

"Eric Liddell. I am a Christian pastor, who rides throughout Hopei to bring the hope of Jesus Christ to all those who will listen."

The soldier chuckled harshly.

"Your place of birth?"

"Tientsin, China," Mu Shi said with a little nod. "I suppose you expected something more like Drymen, Scotland? Ahh, that's where my family's from."

The Japanese seemed both irritated and amused by the pastor's casual chatter.

"I have pictures of my family." Mu Shi's voice was

bright as he reached toward the inner pocket of his heavy sheepskin coat.

"Stop right there!" The younger soldier showed his gun. "We don't like tricks!"

Mu Shi calmly held up his hands while the older soldier roughly frisked him for hidden weapons. Then, unbuttoning Mu Shi's coat, he put his own hand into the inner pocket.

"My wallet," Mu Shi said casually. "Open it. You will see the pictures in there."

Kwei Er saw his pastor raise his head toward heaven for a moment while the soldiers sorted through the pictures and papers in the wallet.

"And where is your traveling money?" The older soldier gave him a smile of superiority.

Mu Shi smiled back at him. "What I have I need. Though it is very little. Please—"

"Take off that coat."

Mu Shi did as he was told.

"I want to see right down to your shirt."

Kwei Er huddled closer to Uncle while Mu Shi stripped off his sweater. The soldier frisked Mu Shi's arms and chest.

"Take off your shoes and socks!" the same soldier demanded, while he nodded for the other man to check for hidden pockets sewn into the coat. Mu Shi waited in his bare feet while the men removed the one paper bill hidden in the toe of the pastor's shoe.

The older soldier drew himself closer. "You *are* a poor pastor! Why don't you go back to the homeland of your parents! Or perhaps you lack the skill or the brains to make a living in the rich lands of Europe."

While Mu Shi was silent, Uncle squeezed Kwei Er close to himself. "Ahh! He is one of the most respected men in his country, that's what Li Mu Shi is!"

A glance from the Japanese silenced Uncle's quiet fretting.

"Get dressed, *mu shi!*" The younger soldier snickered at the title while the older soldier spoke. "China does not seem to care that foreigners come to twist their superstitious ears. But be warned! Japan cares! If we find you on the road again, Eric Liddell, we will make our second meeting with you much less pleasant than the first."

While Mu Shi tied his shoes, the younger soldier flipped the pastor's wallet and Bible over his right shoulder. The wind tossed Mu Shi's papers everywhere. One of his small, stiff photographs tumbled end over end, coming to rest in the dust close to Kwei Er's knee.

The smiling faces of Li Mu Shi's wife and two little daughters looked skyward as Kwei Er reached for the picture.

"The man can pick up his own pictures," the soldiers growled. "We can wait." But soon they were sighing angrily as Mu Shi carefully combed the road and the weeds for every piece of paper that had been thrown to the wind. His patience outlasted the soldiers'. He was still working when the Japanese returned to their trucks and roared away over the hills.

Mu Shi waited for the yellow dust to settle into the wide tracks left by the tires. Then he rushed over, hugging Kwei Er and Uncle as he pulled them to their feet. "I saw you in trouble from the crest of the hill. I didn't know what to do. But when the soldiers stopped me and threw away my things, I took it to be help from God. I knew the Japanese might not harm you as long as foreign eyes were here to watch what happened."

"God gives you so much wisdom and steady courage in every situation!" Uncle marveled.

"Then you are not afraid to go on for me?" Mu Shi asked hopefully.

"Afraid? Ahh, yes! I am afraid." Uncle shared the sparkle Mu Shi had in his own eyes. "But seeing God at work in this danger makes me more certain than ever that you are right in going for this man."

Mu Shi shrugged with delight. "Ma Chuang Fu! You are ready to lead God's church! You have grown spiritual eyes and ears that understand the Holy Spirit's workings. And you know more scripture by heart than I do myself. Just one thing remains undone, I think—"

"I know what you think!" Uncle broke in. "You want me to learn to read and write like some smooth-handed scholar."

Mu Shi chuckled and nodded.

Uncle was firm. "Mu Shi, God provided you as our leader. You bring the Word of God to us. We are just poor peasant workers. We listen to your teaching, and we do for God what you decide is right to do."

For the first time ever, Kwei Er saw sadness cloud Mu Shi's face. "Didn't you hear the Japanese? What they say is true, you know. Sometime, some day, I may be killed or sent out of this country because of my faith. And you, Ma Chuang Fu? You must be ready to help God's people in that day."

Uncle shook his head. "Do not talk of this. Your

father led the church of Siaochang before you. When you are too old to work, God will provide your son to lead us."

Mu Shi broke out laughing. "You know my family! God gave me two daughters!" Then with a serious eye, he looked at the sun in the sky. "How can we get that mule of yours back here?" he asked. "We are short on time."

Uncle sighed, looking out across the field. "When P'ing Tan breaks away like that, it is impossible to catch him. If we had food we might coax him to return. As it is, we will just have to wait until he comes to us."

Li Mu Shi took off his coat. "Watch and pray," he said with a twinkle in his eye. "Perhaps I can get around the other side of him and drive him back in this direction."

Kwei Er's mouth dropped open as he watched Mu Shi take off in a run, making a huge circle around the dark spot that was P'ing Tan grazing far out in the field.

Despite his worry, Uncle chuckled. "You are watching one of the fastest men on earth, my nephew. Do you think it sad that only we, and our mule, and the angels of heaven stand watching?"

Kwei Er looked over to question the meaning of Uncle's words. But he silenced himself, seeing that Uncle found great pleasure in watching his younger friend run.

Suddenly P'ing Tan's hoofbeats sounded close again. Without instruction, Kwei Er leaped out at the same moment Uncle did. P'ing Tan was trapped in front of them for a second, and Uncle grabbed his rope.

Mu Shi came up panting beside Kwei Er. "I'm a

little out of practice, I would say." He beamed at Uncle, sharing more of the secret humor Kwei Er found hard to understand.

"Thank you!" Uncle told him. "God has his reasons for having you here, Mu Shi." Then worry sealed his lips, as Uncle looked at the sky.

"You think we cannot reach Huo Chu by nightfall because of this delay?" the pastor asked.

"I know it." Uncle ran his finger down P'ing Tan's nose. "I have traveled this road thousands of times before, and darkness and bandits can do nothing but increase the distance of a familiar road."

Mu Shi smiled. "Then keep my coat. It only slows me down. My bike is in good condition. I will ride on ahead of you. I will get to Huo Chu before the gates close at dusk. With God's help, I will convince the gatekeeper to let you in when you arrive."

Uncle nodded. "I know your strength. I can think of no better plan."

Mu Shi tapped Kwei Er's shoulder. "Remember," he said, " 'The one who trusts in God will never be put to shame.' " Then he went to pick up his bicycle. Putting one foot against the pedal, he waved and sped away.

Kwei Er heard Uncle whispering, *"I Lu P'ing An!"*

Without a word they hitched P'ing Tan to the cart as quickly as they could. Kwei Er ran beside the mule until he felt he might collapse from the burning in his lungs. Despite his hurry, they found themselves only as far as the leaning tamarisk when the sun touched the earth. They stopped to pray, while they still had light.

4

THE TEMPLE OF DESPAIR

As they raced toward Huo Chu, the sky turned orange, then purple, then black as a lacquered box inlaid with silver stars. Uncle stripped off his robe, exposing his old jacket and trousers to the moonless night. He held P'ing Tan's rope. Kwei Er stayed at his side. Too tense for conversation, they listened for robbers and soldiers as they felt their way along the lightless road.

Finally a haze of lanternlight glowed before them above the square silhouette of village walls. "It is Huo Chu," Uncle whispered. "How thankful I am to God!"

Even P'ing quickened his tired steps, and soon Uncle was pounding on the village gate.

"Go away! Huo Chu is locked until dawn!"

The harsh voice inside the gate turned Kwei Er's eyes to Uncle. By the light seeping through the cracks in the wood, he watched Uncle's cheek twitching with tension. "I want to speak with the Christian missionary, Eric Liddell," Uncle called, his tongue faltering at the hard sounds in Mu Shi's foreign name.

The silence that followed caused Kwei Er to breathe in fearfully.

"Ma Chuang Fu!" It was Mu Shi's voice. "Have patience! Now that you are here, I know this gatekeeper will believe my story is true."

Kwei Er put his ear to the gate to hear every word spoken on the other side. The harsh voice shouted again. "Why should I trust you, a foreigner, and this unknown voice that comes here with the night?"

"Because I know this man. It is his voice!" Mu Shi insisted. "Everything I told you is true."

The gatekeeper laughed loudly. "You, a foreign devil, can tell one Chinese voice from another? I think it a trick." Then the man called loudly, "Go away! I am paid to keep the gate closed until dawn!"

Kwei Er shivered. "What are we to do, Uncle? Even Mu Shi will suffer. We have his coat."

A slow grin came to Uncle's face. "Yes, that is right!" He pressed his cheek against the gate. "Listen!" he said, speaking through the cracks. "Make us prey for the bandits, if you must. But open the gate long enough to take the missionary's coat from us."

Kwei Er heard excitement in Li Mu Shi's voice. "Yes! He does have my coat! That proves we know each other! It is a sheepskin one with a Chinese Bible and a compass in the right outer pocket. And in the inner pocket, there is a wallet with four photographs of my wife and two little girls."

Slowly one side of the gate creaked backward. The dark barrel of a rifle appeared. The face of a young Chinese soldier followed it. "Give me the coat!"

As soon as Uncle held it out, the soldier grabbed it. The gate slammed shut.

Kwei Er bit his lip, while Uncle said a prayer.

The gate creaked again. Moments later they were inside, exchanging grins with Li Mu Shi. After thanking the guard many times for his kindness, Uncle led them to the inn where he and Kwei Er often spent the nights on their way to or from the northern cities.

The innkeeper, a withered, beardless man, welcomed them kindly, until he saw Li Mu Shi. "I have nothing against such men," he whispered privately to Uncle as he kept one eye on the pastor's foreign face. "But these are bad times. Who knows, either the Japanese or the Chinese could take action against me for housing a foreigner."

Uncle took the thin man by the elbow. Walking him around his own courtyard, Uncle bent his ear with secret words. By the time they were back at the gate again, the innkeeper was actually smiling. "Ahh, forgive my delay," he said nervously. "I was merely concerned that a man of your importance would not wish to sleep with carters. You see, I have no private rooms."

Mu Shi's eyebrows raised in wild surprise. Uncle only smiled. They had no time to speak just then. Uncle freed P'ing Tan. While he took the harness and cart to the side of the courtyard, Kwei Er led the mule through the door into the main room of the inn. A large trough ran along the right wall of the smoky, dimly lighted room. Kwei Er found a place for P'ing at the end of the row of mules already there.

When P'ing's great black body had cooled from his

long day of work, Kwei Er brought him water. Then taking the coin Mother had hidden in his shoe, Kwei Er bought a can of dried beans from the innkeeper for P'ing Tan's supper. Getting the food into P'ing's mouth required that Kwei Er stand guard beside him. Each time the neighboring mules' noses came too close to P'ing's section of the trough, Kwei Er knocked them away so that P'ing could eat.

When his work was done, Kwei Er joined Uncle and Mu Shi who were resting near the doorway on the raised brick *k'ang*. The platform covered with dingy quilts served both as a sitting place and as a sleeping area for all the carters crowded into the room. The smell of mules and sweaty men faded from Kwei Er's nose as Uncle handed him a piece of Aunt's bao tyus and a bowl of steaming noodles. "How is it that we have supper?" Kwei Er asked excitedly.

Uncle's eyes twinkled. "You remember that Aunt spoke of Yao's wife's special filling in the dumpling? Why, as I hoped, it was money, enough to buy us all something to eat."

Gratefully Kwei Er sat crosslegged between Uncle and Mu Shi. The k'ang, warmed by small, internal fires, soothed his weary legs and feet. He ate, while Uncle and Mu Shi reviewed the day's events. "Now," the pastor said putting his hands together. "We are to the place where I can ask how you changed the innkeeper's mind."

Uncle drew his lips together. "You will not like it, Mu Shi."

"I can't believe you would lie or bribe!" Mu Shi exclaimed. "I have known you from my childhood. You are slow to speak of Jesus Christ by name, but you never waver from living out your faith in God."

"Ahh, I do not fear that my words to the innkeeper displeased God!" Uncle laughed. "Only you!"

Mu Shi's round eyes narrowed, as they often did at Uncle's teasing. "Then I will try not to be displeased." He smiled.

Still, Uncle seemed nervous about going on. "You see, I told him that if he turned you away, he would miss the opportunity to host one of the fastest men in the world."

Mu Shi cleared his throat. "I have told you not to speak of this. What is past is past."

Uncle showed his toothless grin. "In China we see the past as being part of the present," he said. "You see, I told him that almost every one in your homeland can tell many truths about you. I proved it to him by saying a few of them myself just as your honorable mother originally told them to me."

"What could you tell him that he would understand?"

Uncle closed his eyes. "In 1924 it took you only forty-seven and six-tenth seconds to win a 400-meter footrace in the city of Paris, France." Uncle opened his eyes and grinned.

"He could understand none of that!" Mu Shi protested. "In fact, I'm amazed that you remembered any of those facts yourself."

"Oh, I remember all of your mother's stories about your fantastic running," Uncle said. "And like the innkeeper, I look at you and I am amazed that you live in China now."

Mu Shi laughed self-consciously. He wrinkled his forehead at Kwei Er. "I hope he doesn't bore you with such tales."

Uncle answered for him. "I would like to speak of these stories often," he said. "But I do not, out of respect for your way of thinking that the past is past."

Mu Shi seemed touched by Uncle's words. "The scripture says, 'Let him who boasts boast in the Lord.'"

Uncle nodded. "I know the scripture. I just wish you would understand that when I boast of you, I *am* boasting in the Lord. God made you strong, and wise, and kind. And then after doing all of this, he sent you to China." Uncle's eyes were misty. "I think of this every day, Mu Shi, and I thank God that you are here."

Kwei Er saw Mu Shi swallow hard. "Ahh, it is a blessing from God to be here." He paused. "Well, we are between two long days. Tomorrow we must go to the temple at Pei Lin Tyu. It saddens me to think that we are warm and well fed, while the soldier we come to rescue must stay out in the cold again tonight."

"But back in Siaochang, we agreed it would endanger everyone to rescue the man and bring him here." Uncle reminded him. "By tomorrow night, God willing, we will have him in your doctors' care."

"What if he has moved on—or even died?" Kwei Er asked, breaking from his drowsiness as his empty bowl slipped from his lap.

"All the details we must commit to God," Mu Shi said.

Uncle lowered his voice, though the innkeeper was gone and the other carters were asleep and snoring. "I heard much news in the courtyard this evening. The roads swarm with Japanese. What if we are stopped to-morrow when we have the Chinese soldier in our care? What then?"

Mu Shi sighed. "I don't know. I've been asking God for guidance, but I haven't come up with any answer to that." In silence the pale-haired man wrapped his coat around his shoulders. He stretched out on the k'ang. Uncle lay down on the other side of Kwei Er, who sat watching and thinking about each man as he drifted off to sleep. Soon weariness caused Kwei Er to curl up between them. Though bedbugs pricked his wrists and ankles, the warm bricks under him drew him down into a deep and quiet sleep.

Sometime later in the night, the sound and smell of a sputtering oil lamp awakened him. Kwei Er opened his eyes, but lay still until he could identify the source of the worried conversation traveling back and forth above his head.

"Before I learned of Jesus Christ, I had a slippery tongue." Uncle's voice was muffled to the quietest of whispers. "Perhaps just this once, Mu Shi, God would allow me to weave a tale if the enemy stops us. The man in our cart could be my brother, injured by a mule . . . just to throw the Japanese off our tracks."

By the light of the burning oil lamp on the k'ang, Kwei Er saw Mu Shi shake his head. "Though this rescue might cost our lives, Chuang Fu, God's word clearly says that we must not lie."

Behind him Kwei Er could hear Uncle sigh. "I should not have brought my nephew. Back at Nan Kung, I should have been bolder and trusted God more so that I could have walked to Huo Chu without him. I could be bolder now if I did not have to worry about the safety of this most cherished boy."

Mu Shi looked down to catch Kwei Er's opened eyes. "God can still work his will among us," he said, not letting on that he knew Kwei Er was listening. "After all, he loves Kwei Er even more than you do, Chuang Fu."

"We trust God, yet we lie awake," Uncle whispered back. "What does God want us to do?"

"Perhaps pray or read from the scripture," Mu Shi suggested. "Or maybe we are just awake because of a war of worry that is raging deep within us, where it should not be. When I asked you to come, I did not know the Japanese would be so close."

"Should we go back without the man?" Uncle asked.

Mu Shi blew out a sigh. He reached into his pocket, then bent close to the wavering light. "Sometimes when I am unsure of God's will, I just start reading through the scriptures. As I go, I pray that God will direct me to just the right words of encouragement or instruction."

Even as he spoke Kwei Er saw Mu Shi's finger move down the pages. Soon the tightness around the pastor's eyes was easing. "Listen to this, Chuang Fu! My hand is on the Gospel of Luke, chapter 16, at the tenth verse. 'Whoever can be trusted with very little can also be trusted with much. And those who are dishonest with very little will also be dishonest with much. So if you have not been trustworthy in handling worldly wealth, who will trust you with true riches?'" Mu Shi looked up. "What do you think? That speaks to me."

Kwei Er dared to roll over to see Uncle's face. "God

has been faithful to us, as we have been faithful to him," Uncle observed. "Tomorrow, even bigger trials may come. Then we should expect even more grace to face them, according to God's will."

"Yes, I think that is right," Mu Shi agreed with delight. "Be honest. Be straight in our answers. These are two things we can do. Everything else must be left to God."

Uncle nodded. "It sounds simple, if we can just keep trusting him." For the first time he noticed Kwei Er's gaze. "You have been awake, too? Are you fearful about tomorrow?"

Kwei Er shook his head dreamily. Truthfully, after listening to what had been said, he was not frightened at all. Mu Shi blew out the lamp, and soon after that all of them were sound asleep.

Kwei Er awoke the next morning, full of nervous excitement. He could tell by Mu Shi's open Bible that the men had been studying and praying. "We let you sleep because you were awake so long last night," Uncle explained as he pressed a bowl of hot water into Kwei Er's hand. Kwei Er drank it quickly, knowing that this could be his only breakfast since their last coin had already been spent.

Other carters stirred around them. As soon as Kwei Er's bowl was empty, he handed it to Uncle. After combing his hair with his fingers and smoothing his clothes with his hands, he went across the room to P'ing Tan.

Uncle had the cart ready when Kwei Er brought P'ing into the courtyard. The sky was a pearly gray by the time they had P'ing in harness. Uncle spoke to several other carters to get information about the village and the temple of Pei Lin Tyu. Then he shared with Mu Shi the distances and directions to several places in and near the town.

"I will ride the nine li to the headman's house," Mu Shi decided when Uncle finished his talk. "I will tell the local official that we wish to take a Chinese soldier from his town so he can be treated at the hospital of Siao-chang. If we have the headman's permission no one, except those who support the Japanese, will have reason to distrust us."

Uncle nodded. "While you do this, Kwei Er and I will head directly for the temple. Today it will be crowded with people burning their New Year's offerings. No one will take notice of us, until you come, Mu Shi. But by then, we will know the location and the condition of the man we came to help."

"Good!" The pastor took up his bicycle. "God willing, we will see each other soon at the temple of Pei Lin Tyu."

Uncle watched Mu Shi with open admiration as the man cycled out into the street. Then they, too, went out through the courtyard gate. Dark clouds clung to the rooftops of the village like low dense wads of cotton. "It looks like the New Year will be blessed with the snow that makes good harvest!" a man with a carrying pole called out cheerfully as he squeezed by them in the narrow street. But Kwei Er felt the corners of his own mouth turning down. Snow would only make the trip back colder and more troublesome. Uncle said nothing, but hurried P'ing through the West gate, which the carters had said would set them on the shortest route to Pei Lin Tyu.

Sooner than Kwei Er expected it, Uncle was pointing out the temple rising in the distance. Walls of rough clay supported the faded tile roof pressed against the sky. Uncle left P'ing Tan outside one of the temple's red gates. They followed on the heels of the earliest of worshipers as they walked inside. Whirlwinds of dust twisted around Kwei Er's ankles as cold drafts blew in and out of the wide temple doorways. Long-robed priests thrust unlighted incense sticks in his direction, but Uncle pulled Kwei Er past these men into the cold, dark interior.

The smoke of incense clung to their hair and clothes like sticky cobwebs. Everywhere Kwei Er turned, the unseeing eyes of metal and earth idols stared out at him. Every few moments the faces of the buddhas and the gods grew bright as paper offerings were set afire in braziers placed around the eerie room.

These sights and smells brought back memories of Kwei Er's earliest childhood along the Grand Canal. But instead of feeling awed by the temple, Kwei Er sensed a hollow, sadness now. He shivered to think that the man they were searching for had lain in this cold, forsaken place for five days.

Suddenly Uncle squeezed his wrist. Turning from the idols, Kwei Er saw what Uncle saw—some movement on the floor. Taking a step closer, Kwei Er gasped at the sight of a rat scurrying away from the form of a man stretched out on the clay. At first Kwei Er was certain this had to be the carved image of a man. The skin he saw was white as porcelain. The lips and hands were icy blue.

But Uncle crouched beside the figure. He laid a finger against the nostrils of the human form. "He's breathing," Uncle said. "Hopefully we've come in time to save him."

The man's eyes fluttered at Uncle's touch and voice.

"Don't be afraid," Uncle whispered. "We are here to help. I am a mule carter. This is my nephew. We know a Christian missionary who wants to take you to a warm hospital in Siaochang where you can get medical treatment."

The man rolled his eyes in distress. He moved his lips, but made no sound.

"You wish to go?" Uncle guessed.

Slowly the man lowered his chin, then raised it again.

Uncle touched his arm. "Rest. As soon as the man named Li Mu Shi comes here, we will carry you to my cart." Uncle looked at Kwei Er. "Go watch for Mu Shi. When he comes, direct him inside. But you stay with P'ing Tan. We risk having him stolen each moment he is left alone."

Kwei Er avoided looking at the idols again as he wove out through the ever-thickening, incoming crowd. He had taken only a few breaths of fresh air beside P'ing Tan when he saw Mu Shi pushing his bicycle to the gate. Immediately the pastor came to his side.

"We have found him!" Kwei Er said excitedly.

Mu Shi turned his head away. "I hear everything you say, Kwei Er. But do not look so eager to talk with me. I have only kind words to report from the headman of the village. Still there is troubling news. I have been followed here by a short Chinese peasant who carries his left arm in a sling."

Kwei Er, tense with the realization of new danger, made himself pick burrs from P'ing's short mane. His voice trembled. "Uncle waits inside for you. The man lies in one of the corners farthest from the door."

Mu Shi shared a quick smile with him. "Be careful as you wait alone. Don't talk to any man." Then before Kwei Er risked a nod, Mu Shi parked his bicycle along the temple wall and disappeared within the crowd.

There was no way to keep all eyes from turning on them when Uncle and Mu Shi carried out the limp soldier a few moments later. As they laid him into the cart, Uncle whispered to Kwei Er. "Turn P'ing back toward Huo Chu at once, in case there are those in this crowd who favor Japan's rule."

But Kwei Er could not even lead P'ing away from the wall because of the curious onlookers pressed all around them. Suddenly Kwei Er's stomach was in his throat. A short Chinese man with his arm in a sling watched them from the crowd.

"Mu Shi, the man you worry about is here!" Kwei Er choked. But the sound of his voice was lost as the temple visitors began to shout both encouragements and threats at them for daring to move the soldier.

As the commotion increased, Mu Shi jumped up onto the cart shaft and raised his hands. "I have permission from the headman of your village to move this man for treatment in a hospital. You must move back so that we can get through to the road. You see for yourself that his condition is critical. We must leave at once, to give him every chance for life."

The mood of the crowd changed at Mu Shi's words. Tearful cries and words of gratefulness wove around them. Many who were closest to them lighted their incense sticks as a sign that they wanted their prayers to go heavenward for the injured man.

As the bittersweet smoke drifted into Kwei Er's face, he saw tears welling up in Mu Shi's pale eyes. "Listen, all of you," Mu Shi cried out. "The fresh air that is given by the Creator of Heaven and Earth himself is better for this man than your smoking incense. If it was not urgent for us to go for help, I would stay to tell you many things about the true Word of God that is written in this book."

Looking down at the Bible now in his hands, Mu Shi went on. "There have been others just like you who ask, 'With what shall I come before the Lord and bow down before the exalted God? Shall I come before Him with burnt offerings, . . . or with ten thousand rivers of oil?' Listen to the answer God has written for us here. 'The Lord himself has showed you what is good. And what does He require of you? To act justly. To love mercy. And to walk humbly with Him as your only God.'"

While Mu Shi spoke, Kwei Er's eyes begged Uncle for his attention. "Mu Shi told me he is being followed!" Kwei Er whispered when Uncle finally leaned close to him. "And I have seen the man. His arm is in a sling. He is right over there." But when Kwei Er's glance floated to where the man had been, his mouth went dry. "He is gone!"

Uncle put his hand on Mu Shi's knee as he stood above the crowd. "Come down, my friend!" Uncle urged. "Another day, preach to these people. We must get away."

Reluctantly, Mu Shi accepted Uncle's counsel and climbed down from the cart. But as he grabbed his bicycle and came back to Uncle, Kwei Er heard him sigh. "We can never assume there will be another day, Chuang Fu. Christ calls us to speak of him to others while we have today."

"I know," Uncle said. He seemed lost in thought as he put his hand to P'ing's halter and quickly circled the cart around. All those who had been reluctant to move back now jumped away as Uncle trotted his big mule down to the street. Kwei Er struggled to keep pace with Uncle's quick-stepped run and Mu Shi's gliding speed on his bicycle.

By the time Uncle slowed the pace, they were far away from Pei Lin Tyu. "We will take this road to the West gate of Huo Chu," Uncle panted. "There we will turn south along the wall, instead of going through the village. This way there will be fewer people to notice us, and the carters assured me this morning that this route also connects with the road to Siaochang."

Uncle's plan seemed good until they reached the West gate. As they turned south, suddenly a Chinese soldier crossed their path. Though his rifle was locked in his hands, the man was smiling. "Do you remember me?" he asked. "I am the guard from last night."

Mu Shi stopped, straddling his bike. "Yes, of course."

"I have watched for you all morning. From your talk in the courtyard, the innkeeper guessed you would come this way."

Kwei Er tensed, realizing it was not good for their

route of travel to be so freely known. Still Mu Shi kept smiling, nodding for the man to go on speaking.

"I hope you don't mind. The innkeeper told all about you. I just wanted to apologize for how difficult I made things for you last night."

Mu Shi nodded politely. "Thank you for taking time to meet us again. But you must know that in God's eyes we all are of equal importance."

The soldier, so interested in conversation, suddenly seemed distracted from Mu Shi's words. "Japanese trucks coming this way!" he whispered breathlessly. "They must not see you hauling that Chinese soldier. Quick! Through the village and out the North gate. Take the first road to your right, and several li beyond that crossroad, you will find yourself heading south again."

5

A Fear of Things to Come

Ping Tan's hoofs pounded on the streets of Huo Chu. The cart rattled behind Kwei Er and Uncle as Li Mu Shi sped ahead of them on his bicycle. None of them dared to look back until they had slipped through the North gate. As soon as they were out of the village, they paused long enough to decide what to do.

"You go on, Mu Shi!" Uncle urged. "Maybe Kwei Er and I will not be stopped if we are seen without you."

"But what about the soldier?" Mu Shi countered quickly. "What will you do if you are caught and questioned?"

"We will hide the man as well as we can," Uncle replied. "Hopefully we will not be stopped. The road seems deserted. Any who are on it will think we are just two ordinary workers heading out after a night at the muleteers' inn."

Mu Shi nodded reluctantly. "All right. I will wait for you at the crossroads," he promised. "If you are delayed, I will come back to find you."

Fear tugged at Kwei Er as Mu Shi pedaled away.

Uncle covered the injured soldier's face with one quilt. "Stay very still," he said to the half-conscious man. "We have escaped the Japanese so far. God watches over us, I am sure." Then Uncle grabbed P'ing Tan's lead, and Kwei Er's feet soon found the rhythm of the older carter's short quick steps.

The danger they were in made Kwei Er strong and alert. He raced beside the mule, feeling that tiredness would never catch him again. They were the only ones on the road. Soon Huo Chu was far behind them and Uncle slowed their pace. Gratefully Kwei Er breathed in the air of freedom that hung between the gray clouds and the open fields. Before they started their mule trotting again, Uncle spoke a prayer of thanks to God for allowing them to once more escape their enemies.

Then with renewed courage, they traveled even more quickly down the road. Kwei Er sneaked a grin at Uncle because of the fast pace they were keeping. But when he looked out at the road again, Kwei Er was shocked to see Mu Shi waving his hands. "Slow down!" the pastor cried.

P'ing, still edgy from the confusion at Huo Chu, bolted forward instead of stopping. Uncle pulled at him and Kwei Er screamed. The moment before the mule collided with Mu Shi, the pastor yanked his bicycle away and leaped to the side of the road. The moment after that, the mule brayed with surprise as the roadway swallowed him up to his chest in loose soil. He snorted and rolled his eyes wildly, trying to pull himself out of the well of soft dirt. Kwei Er and Uncle jumped in beside him on the plowed up road. They sank almost to their waists as they reached out to soothe the distressed mule.

"Easy! Easy!" Uncle said, floundering as though he waded in deep sand or snow instead of dirt. Each time P'ing tossed his head, the cart tottered dangerously close to the edge of the firm road, threatening to spill the injured man onto the dug-out roadbed.

With patience and many quiet words, Uncle and Kwei Er finally worked P'ing Tan back onto the last undamaged portion of the road. Mu Shi came to them as Uncle brushed away the loose soil clinging to P'ing Tan's quivering hide. "The whole road has been destroyed by Japanese bombs," Mu Shi explained with a sigh. "I traveled farther to have a look, and there are shell holes ahead deep enough to swallow up P'ing Tan *and* his cart."

Uncle's eyes went out over the landscape. "Then we'll turn off here and head south on our own. Unless it rains or snows, the fields should be firm enough to hold us."

Mu Shi glanced at the cloudy sky. "Let's stay together," he suggested. "I have a compass. That will help find our way." Before they turned off the road, Uncle and Mu Shi checked the soldier in the cart. "The man has quite a fever." Kwei Er heard concern in Mu Shi's voice. "We must get to Siaochang as quickly as we can."

Uncle nodded. There was sadness in his eyes. "I am afraid that I am responsible for this trouble," Uncle said. "This morning I was thrilled that the gatekeeper came to speak with you because of my conversation with the innkeeper of Huo Chu. Now, however, I am worried. Certainly a gatekeeper would know the condition of the roadways around his village. I fear he has betrayed us. Perhaps he directed us this way just so the Japanese could capture us out here without anyone's knowing it."

"Or maybe he truly is a friend," Mu Shi countered gently, "one who knows that these road conditions will keep all Japanese troops from coming our way."

The lines across Uncle's forehead softened. "I hope you are right, Mu Shi."

Kwei Er noticed P'ing Tan's ears prick forward. The mule looked behind him, as though he, too, worried that they were being trailed by the Japanese. Suddenly Kwei Er saw what P'ing Tan was watching. "It's the man with the sling!" Kwei Er gasped. "Quick! We must get out of here!"

Mu Shi touched his arm. "Wait! He is too close now. It is impossible to avoid him. Let him confront us if he wants to, and we will be honest and straightforward in our answers—just as we said we would be last night."

A breeze tousled Mu Shi's thin hair as he steadily watched the man come to him. Kwei Er felt himself stiffen as the stranger stopped. The man, wearing dark trousers and coat, had small black eyes that moved in all directions. He looked at Mu Shi, at Uncle, at Kwei Er.

"You are Li Mu Shi from the Jesus Mission station at Siaochang," the stranger said directing his eyes to the pastor.

"Yes?" Mu Shi nodded.

"The gatekeeper at Huo Chu said I would find you here."

"It is as I feared," Uncle breathed aloud. "This man and the other are working together."

The stranger shot an uncertain glance at Uncle. "We are friends. That is all. Until the Japanese took our town, I served as a guard for the next village east of Huo Chu." He stared into Mu Shi's face. "Since you left Pei Lin Tyu this morning, I have been following you."

"Yes, I know," Mu Shi said calmly.

"After seeing the headman at Pei Lin Tyu, you went to the temple to get the soldier who now lies under the quilt in this cart. You know the Japanese forbid this sort of action. How dare you break the rules?"

Mu Shi hesitated, though he did not look away. "Because rules of God are better than the rules of men," he said finally. "I want to live to honor God, and according to the Word of God written in the sacred scriptures, we are required to help anyone who is in need."

The man stepped closer to Mu Shi. Kwei Er saw a pistol resting deep within his sling. "Mu Shi! Be careful!" Kwei Er cried with instant terror.

"Why are you following me?" Mu Shi asked, his eyes calm and his chin steady.

Unexpectedly, the other man answered with pleading words. "You must come with me, Mu Shi. The moment you left the headman at Pei Lin Tyu, he assigned me to follow you. He needed to know if you would really have the courage to rescue the man in the temple, as you said you would." The stranger lowered his voice to a whisper. "Now that we know you can be trusted, I beg you to come with me. There is a second wounded man who needs your help."

"Who?" Mu Shi asked.

"A well-respected, skilled artist from my village." The man bit his lip. "When the Japanese took our town, they forced many who were educated to kneel down before them in the streets. Then, after all the peasants were

rounded up to watch, the Japanese soldiers cut off the head of each man who knelt."

Kwei Er grabbed Uncle's hand to give himself courage.

"The man who survives would not bow down." The stranger's voice faltered. "While he stood, a Japanese officer cut his throat. Hours later, some of us risked going to bury these men. That is when we discovered this man Xin Shen was still alive."

Mu Shi winced with compassion. "Our cart is small. I don't even know if we can take a second passenger, especially one with such a serious wound."

"Please," the man begged. "He lies between life and death where we have hidden him. Please, come and see what you can do."

Uncle gave Mu Shi a look of warning. "This could still be a trap!" he whispered. "Perhaps this stranger wants to draw you back to Japanese officials."

Mu Shi shook his head. "I think we should go. We have tried to be faithful in small things. Now we must be faithful in this bigger task."

The man turned them east, leading them across many fields and ditches. A flurry of hard snowflakes crackled down against their eyes and lips. A new wave of uncertainty climbed Kwei Er's spine when he saw the Japanese flag waving over the gates of the stranger's village. He pressed himself against Uncle's arm. "Do you think it is a trap?" he whispered frantically.

"I don't know," Uncle admitted. "But it is too late to turn around."

Their guide paused as they brought the cart into town. He looked left and right in the quiet streets. At a moment when no one was moving between houses, he took them quickly into a courtyard hidden behind a tall mud wall.

Kwei Er noticed that the double poverty of winter and war had not completely erased the former beauty of the garden they had entered. The graceful branches of a small bare tree curved over the frozen circle of a goldfish pool. Instead of packed clay, their feet—even P'ing's—walked on well-made bricks.

Their unnamed leader motioned for them to wait outside doors that were decorated with lacy patterns carved in wood. A hundred questions throbbed in Kwei Er's head, but he was silent even when the man with the sling came back to call them in. Reluctantly Uncle dropped P'ing Tan's rope. Mu Shi leaned his bicycle against the wall. He took off his coat and put it across the wounded soldier's chest to give him added warmth before he followed Uncle and Kwei Er into the house.

Paper windows bathed the wide low room in an icy-colored light. Two men with long faces and thin beards watched them come in. By their smooth skin and fine clothes, Kwei Er guessed that they were wealthy, educated men. One continued to stand, while the other sat down on a carved wooden seat. "You are the missionary Li Mu Shi?" the seated man asked.

"Yes," the pastor answered, walking up to him.

The man stared at him. "I know a wealthy man who may wish to entrust you with some grave responsibilities," he said without blinking. "But before I say more, I must know which side you favor in this war."

Kwei Er watched Mu Shi's lips part in thought. "I

am not in China to take political sides. I am here to share the Word of God with anyone who will listen to it."

"Then why do you have that Chinese soldier in the cart outside?" the man asked sharply.

"Sharing God's Word does not just mean speaking it to others," Mu Shi answered steadily. "It means living day by day as God wants us to, and this includes going out of our way to help those who are in need."

"That is your only reason for being here?"

"Yes."

"I have heard enough!" the seated man said abruptly, "Take Li Mu Shi behind the house."

Kwei Er's breath caught in his throat as the second man motioned for Mu Shi to follow him to the door. Boldly Uncle went after them, but the seated man called out, "Carter, you will stay! Mu Shi goes alone."

Uncle turned on his heels, his eyes burning with a passion Kwei Er had never seen before. "Li Mu Shi never goes alone!" Uncle shouted. "God is with him! Don't you try to hurt him or—"

The man in the chair raised his hand. "Nothing like that is planned. I want Li Mu Shi to speak with a friend of mine, now that I am convinced his reasons for the rescue of the first man are purely religious and not political."

Uncle frowned, as though he doubted the speaker's words.

Time moved like a frozen stream, but finally Kwei Er caught a glimpse of Mu Shi's face in the doorway. As the pastor came into the room, safe and sound, Kwei Er could not keep himself from running to his side. "You should not worry about me so much, my young friend," Mu Shi said taking hold of Kwei Er's hand. "The man I just saw is the one who needs our concern now. I am not sure what to do."

"Why is that?" the man in the chair demanded as he rose to his feet. "Why can't you help?"

Mu Shi shook his head. "Your friend Xin Shen believes that foreigners always put their own interests first. The fact that I am willing to take him to Siaochang makes him fear me. From what I can understand of his weak, muffled speech, he believes I want to cheat him out of his wealth by promising him a doctor's help."

The man standing by the chair put his hands together. "We have good reason to mistrust those of your race, Mu Shi. But when we heard you were near our town, we had hope because of the good things we have heard about you. If Xin Shen will not trust you, we have no choice but to keep him hidden in the shed until he dies."

Mu Shi sighed. "The way to Siaochang is very dangerous, and Xin Shen is very ill. I told him I could not promise him safety or health, but I understand why he is reluctant to trust me."

Uncle stepped forward. "If I could speak with Xin Shen for just a few moments, I know I could get him to travel with us."

The two men frowned. "What could you say that this foreigner cannot say for himself?"

Uncle glanced at Mu Shi. "The words I have are for Xin Shen alone," he said. "But I promise you that everything I tell him will be true."

"Let the carter try," the man at the chair advised. "What harm can it do?" His friend shrugged in agreement and led Uncle away. Mu Shi looked at Kwei Er with his calm blue eyes. But before Kwei Er could even think of what to say to him, Uncle was back in the room showing his big toothless grin. "Xin Shen will come," he announced. "We need to find a way to carry him on the cart."

"What did you say?" the man at the chair exclaimed.

Uncle smiled. "Very little," he admitted, "I merely showed him a picture that I carry with me, one that always gives me courage."

The man motioned for Uncle to stand by him. "It is a picture I must see!" he said.

Uncle looked at Mu Shi sheepishly. "Please, do not be disappointed in me again. I tried to honor you, Mu Shi, and I did not boast of you with many words . . . but I did show him this." Slowly Uncle pulled a yellowed patch of newspaper from his inner jacket pocket. Carefully he unfolded it along cracking lines that were brown with age.

"It's a photograph of Mu Shi!" Kwei Er whispered looking over Uncle's shoulder at the picture of a man in short white pants who ran with his face turned up toward the sky.

"Where did you get that!" Mu Shi exclaimed.

Uncle chuckled. "Your honored mother gave it to me as a gift when she left China. For many years I have carried it next to my heart. It is my constant reminder that you gave up fame and comfort in your own country to bring God's Word to China. For me, and now for Xin Shen, this picture is proof that you love God and others more than yourself."

Mu Shi gave a self-conscious sigh. "I thought we agreed that you would tell no more tales about me."

"Yes!" Uncle nodded. "In truth, I said almost nothing." His toothless smile showed again. "But in China, Mu Shi, we have a saying: 'One picture is worth a thousand words!'"

"The important thing is that Xin Shen will go with us," Mu Shi said, changing the subject. "And we must hurry. Outside the sun keeps up its race of time even when we stand talking." Xin Shen's two friends nodded with concern.

In the courtyard, Uncle and Mu Shi found a scrap of wood to make an extra seat for Xin Shen across the cart shafts. Then his two friends carried the wounded man out. They set Xin Shen gently on the plank between the cart shafts, behind P'ing Tan's tail and near the boards that rimmed the cart.

"Are you strong enough to ride this way?" Mu Shi asked.

The thick black rags wrapped around Xin Shen's mouth and neck hampered his speaking. "Yes . . ." he said wearily with his eyes half-closed. "Let us begin at once."

"I will walk beside you," Uncle said to Xin Shen. "If the jolting of the cart is too much for you, tell me and we will stop to let you rest." Then turning to the two local men, Uncle asked for detailed accounts of all the roads leading south. Finally he looked at Kwei Er. "Take P'ing Tan home at your fastest pace. Listen carefully to me as you go. I will help you choose the safest route."

The man with the sling, who had kept watch at the courtyard gate, now sneaked them back into the street. Before Mu Shi put his leg across his bicycle, he paused to speak to the man. "You come, too," he urged. "Let one of the doctors look at your injured arm."

"No, not now," the man answered with a quiet smile. "It is enough for you to try getting two wounded men to safety. I will come to Siaochang as soon I can. I will come to see how Xin Shen is doing. And when he is ready to go home, I will travel with him."

"Perhaps then you will let a doctor have a look at you," Mu Shi said. "I will be praying that we see you soon."

The man with the sling closed the gates of the house behind them. Nervously Kwei Er trotted P'ing Tan out of town. With Mu Shi out in front of him on his bicycle, Kwei Er ran with Uncle's mule until his head pounded and his eyesight dulled with fatigue.

When Uncle finally called for him to take a rest, Kwei Er noticed that snow was falling again. He opened his hot, dry lips to catch a taste of frozen water. For a moment he remembered the happy greeting of the coolie in Huo Chu who hoped for a good harvest because of this New Year's snow. But as he looked back at Uncle his pleasant memory turned to fear.

Their footprints, along with the tracks of the bicycle and the cart, flowed out behind them like unraveling threads. The troublesome sight caused Kwei Er to run again. No matter how carefully Uncle chose their path, he realized that anyone could follow them easily in the wet snow.

6

SEPARATE
WAYS

Hunger and tiredness slowly wove a trap for Kwei Er as he raced P'ing Tan south toward Siaochang. Struggling to keep the pace with Li Mu Shi, who rode the bicycle ahead of him, and Uncle, who ran behind him at Xin Shen's side, Kwei Er forced himself to press on. Then one foot slipped on the sloshy roadway. The other followed it, and the next thing Kwei Er knew he was lying on his back looking straight up into the worried faces of Uncle and his pastor.

Uncle pulled Kwei Er to his feet, while Mu Shi ran to get his coat from the cart. "We are expecting too much of you," Mu Shi said, wrapping his dry sheepskin garment around Kwei Er's shoulders. "You need to rest awhile."

But Kwei Er pulled himself away. Draped in Mu Shi's coat, he grabbed P'ing Tan's lead. "I am fine!" he said. "I can go on!"

"We should take a rest," Uncle told him. "You are almost as pale as the man in the cart."

Kwei Er touched his cheeks in dismay. "We must

go on!" The cry clung to his throat. "We can't all be trapped on the road, just because I am too weak to travel quickly."

"The sun is breaking through the clouds," Uncle said with a sigh of relief. "We wouldn't lose that much time now that the weather is improving. As we rest, the road will dry. That will make it easier to travel when we start again."

Mu Shi put a reassuring hand on Kwei Er's shoulder. "You are doing far more than any other boy I know could do with so little food and rest."

Kwei Er bit his lip to keep the slight grin from showing on his face. "Is it really so, Mu Shi?"

"Of course!" the pastor said, while Uncle nodded. "In fact, we should all rest for a while, and take some time to thank God for getting us this far. If we were in my country right now, the road might be filled with those who had come to watch us on this most unusual race. And do you know what those people probably would be saying to me right now?"

Kwei Er shook his head.

Mu Shi's light eyebrows bent down. He raised his hands, pretending he was confused. Then he spoke in his own language, which none of them could understand.

"There!" he said in Chinese. "That is exactly what they might say!"

Kwei Er giggled, as he always did when Mu Shi entertained them with foreign looks and Western words. "You know we can't understand you when you speak like that."

"Ahh, so now you want a translation?" Mu Shi asked, with a twinkle in his eye.

Kwei Er grinned.

"Well, it would be something like this." Mu Shi raised his hands again. " 'Eric Liddell!' the people would be shouting. 'You're the Olympic runner who refused to race on Sunday. But now, in China, you dare to run on such a day as this?' "

Kwei Er's eyes felt wide. "Mu Shi, is *this* day really Sunday?"

"Yes, it is."

"Then you are running *and* working on Sunday!" Kwei Er exclaimed.

Mu Shi looked at him and at Uncle, too. "Jesus Christ is Lord of the Sabbath. It is not the Sabbath that I wish to honor with my life. It is the Lord of the Sabbath."

Mu Shi's eyes moved to Xin Shen who painfully changed position on his narrow wooden seat. Though the great dark bandages kept his head from turning, the man glanced around fearfully.

Mu Shi went to comfort him. "Can you stand for a moment against me to stretch your legs?" the pastor asked.

"No!" Xin Shen mumbled. "We must go on."

"We can see in all directions here," Mu Shi assured him as Uncle checked the man in the cart. "No one is near us. That is why we rest now."

The man struggled to look at the sky. "It was safer . . . when it snowed. Bad weather keeps away bandits. It slows soldiers down."

Mu Shi nodded. "I have lived in China long enough to know these things. But I also know that God watches over even the things we cannot see. Please, do not worry. I believe God is directing us."

"What is this day you call . . . Sabbath?" Xin Shen asked as Uncle returned to them.

Mu Shi seemed to wait for Uncle to speak, but when he did not, Mu Shi explained. "God made the entire world and everything in it in six days. Then on the seventh day, God rested. When God wrote the ten Great Commandments, he included the instruction that people and their beasts of burden should work for six days only and then rest on the seventh day."

"Your God makes this rule . . . yet you dare to disobey it?" Xin Shen's weary eyes filled with worry. "Then we expect misfortune . . . not divine protection now!"

Mu Shi shook his head. "No, my God is not like that," he said with confidence. "The greatest law of the Lord we serve is the law of love. 'Do good on the Sabbath.' This, also, is recorded in the sacred scriptures."

Xin Shen's head dropped back against the cartboards. "Do good . . . for a stranger?" he mused painfully. "At the risk of your own lives. . . . Why?"

Mu Shi touched the man's knee. "Because you are not a stranger to God, Xin Shen. He made you, he knows you, and he wants you to understand his love."

Xin Shen glanced at Mu Shi with uncertainty.

Suddenly the distant drone of an airplane turned all their faces toward the clouds breaking up against the pale blue sky.

"It's a Japanese plane!" Uncle's voice was hushed with fear.

Mu Shi watched the metal speck in the western sky. "It's some distance away. Perhaps it's covering the movement of troops on another road."

Uncle spoke without taking his eyes from the silver spot in the open clouds. "The men this morning told me of another road that parallels this one for a while. But according to their description, these two roads should come together soon."

"What if the Japanese are heading south as we are?" Kwei Er asked unable to contain his own worry. "They will find us for sure."

Mu Shi looked at Uncle, then at Kwei Er. "You can move faster than the troops," he said. "If that intersection is near here, you will have time to cross before the Japanese even come by there."

"And what of you?" Uncle asked.

"I will follow you through the crossroad. Then I will slow down so that you can be out in front of me. That way, if the Japanese do turn south along the road, they will meet me before they will meet you."

Even Xin Shen was listening carefully to Mu Shi's plan.

"Why do this?" Uncle protested.

"Because you have the wounded men," Mu Shi answered. "If the Japanese stop me, it will give you more time to reach Siaochang."

"But you, Mu Shi!" Kwei Er exclaimed. "I heard them say they will make you suffer greatly if they meet you again."

93

"It is unlikely that I will see the same Japanese soldiers twice," Mu Shi said. "And, besides, I have heard such threats many times before." He touched Kwei Er's head. "We are going to pray right here and now. And I want you to think on this: No Christian can find a safer place to be than at the center of God's will."

The threat of tears stung Kwei Er's eyes as he bowed his head, listening to Mu Shi pray. "Lord, make your will known to us now. We give ourselves to you so that you may lead us and decide what is right for each of us, including Xin Shen and the wounded soldier we desire to take to safety. Even now, Lord, let our greatest joy come from doing what pleases you. In Christ's name, we pray. Amen."

Looking up, Mu Shi squeezed each of their hands. "God be with you, Ma Chuang Fu. God be with you, Kwei Er. And with you, Xin Shen."

"I Lu P'ing An." Uncle's voice trembled. Then he nodded to Kwei Er, who took up P'ing Tan's rope with a weak hand.

Mu Shi pushed his bicycle past him. "You cannot run all the way to Siaochang," his pastor told him calmly. "So you must not think that God desires you to. Instead, go only as quickly as you can, knowing that you have to have enough strength to travel at least two more hours on the road. Don't let fear chase you. That can tire you quickly. Focus on God. Let him be your strength."

Kwei Er drew in a deep breath. "I will try to do what you say."

"I know you will." Mu Shi grinned. "I will ride with you as far as the crossroads to help you set a pace that will take you all the way to Siaochang." With that,

Mu Shi was off. Because of his pastor's confidence in him, Kwei Er felt himself holding his head high. If God planned for him to be leading P'ing Tan now, he thought, there was nothing to fear. With Mu Shi riding at his side, the trip to the crossroads was not worrisome.

But when Mu Shi stopped at the junction and nodded for him to go on alone, Kwei Er fought tears and the temptation to look back. Then Uncle's voice came to him. "Trust in the Lord! Kwei Er, keep going!"

Kwei Er went on at the pace Mu Shi had set for him, making sure his ears always heard the same rhythmic pounding of his feet. He made himself think only that God had kept them safe this far. Perhaps it was his will that they get to the hospital this afternoon.

P'ing Tan trotted as though he, too, sensed an unseen power at work in them. Together they hurried li after li, until the gates of Siaochang actually came into view. Their entrance into the hospital compound was like a dream to Kwei Er. He saw the gatekeeper, the Western doctor, and Chinese helpers rushing down to them from the porch. Only after both wounded men had been whisked away, did Kwei Er blow out a tense sigh to let himself believe that they were really there.

Uncle's hand clamped on his shoulder. "The Lord be praised! The Lord be praised for getting us here."

But Kwei Er's eyes drifted back to the still-opened compound gates. "What of Li Mu Shi?" he said in anguish. "I will not feel fully thankful until he is safely home."

Uncle's dark face was tender. "Mu Shi can be in no better hands right now than God's hands."

Kwei Er nodded in silent agreement. Still he looked

beyond the open gates of Siaochang, hoping to see a man on a bicycle riding in under the golden afternoon sky.

"Wait for him at the gate," Uncle suggested quietly. "I will care for P'ing Tan and then go inside to see Yao Feng and the two others we have just carried here."

With hesitation, Kwei Er walked up to the old gate-keeper who had his eyes on the road. "Do you want something?" the gray-haired man asked when he turned back into the courtyard.

"Oh, no!" Kwei Er answered quickly. "I-I just thought I'd wait for Li Mu Shi to come home."

The gatekeeper's eyes surveyed the yellow fields beyond the compound walls. "I know what it is like to watch for him," the old man said with a thin smile. "The hours in Siaochang are always longer when we are here in safety and he is not."

Kwei Er brushed his cheek. "Then I may wait with you?"

The man nodded with pleasure. "I watched you bring the cart in. I know you are one who dared to go to Huo Chu with Mu Shi. You must be exhausted from the journey. You can rest and wait."

As the gatekeeper spoke, Kwei Er felt his head grow heavy with his tiredness.

The man led him to the side of the gate. "Here, use my stool. Cover yourself with my blanket. You will wait with me." The man's face broke into a smile. "But I will do the watching."

Even though Kwei Er was worried, sleep soon tracked him down. His head had already drifted to the wall when the gatekeeper made him alert again with a small bowl of tea from his own teapot. Kwei Er drank it hastily. He rested his head against the wall again, and this time no one woke him from his sleep.

Much later, he heard someone speak his name.

Looking up, he saw Li Mu Shi's happy face. "So you have been waiting for me?"

Kwei Er brought himself back to reality by rubbing his hand across his face. "Oh, yes! And now you are here!"

Mu Shi pinched his own hand. "Yes, I think I am!"

Suddenly Kwei Er felt ashamed of his worrying. "I am not strong in the ways you are," he said with regret. "I feared something awful would happen to you. I feared I would never see you again."

The gatekeeper walked away as Mu Shi crouched down beside Kwei Er. "I have learned many good Chinese sayings from your Uncle and others. But now, Kwei Er, I have a true saying to teach you. 'Those who love God never meet for the last time.' Even if death should come quickly to one of us, we will not have to fear a last good-bye. For God has planned that Christians will see each other again—in heaven."

Mu Shi stood and gently pulled Kwei Er to his feet. "Your Uncle wants to leave for Nan Kung so that you can be with your family tonight. God willing, I will see you in seven days, when Sunday comes around again."

Kwei Er managed to return Mu Shi's smile. Then with the pastor's hand on his shoulder, he walked to the center of the courtyard where Uncle waited beside P'ing Tan and their cart.

7

THE
PEACEMAKERS

Night was on their heels as they came to Nan Kung. In the dusky light of the day's last shadows, Uncle knocked at his own courtyard gate. "Welcome home!" Yao's son shouted, throwing open the entryway. Kwei Er hurried in, happy for safety and rest.

But suddenly his arm jerked as P'ing Tan stopped abruptly at the other end of the lead rope. Uncle joined Kwei Er to pull, to swat, to plead, but the mule would not go into the courtyard.

"If it is the hen that worries him, she is not here," Yao's son volunteered sadly. "Soon after we locked her in the garden that first day, she disappeared."

Uncle looked from the disappointed boy to the stubborn mule for a moment. Then he began trying to move P'ing Tan again. "Get up, you!" he growled. "We have already lost the chicken. I am not about to let you get away, too."

Kwei Er's sisters suddenly encircled them. "Welcome home, Uncle! And Brother! And P'ing Tan!" Cautiously, First Younger Sister held out a hand to the balky mule. "P'ing Tan, here is a gift for you," she said nervously. To Kwei Er's surprise, she had a long carrot in her fist. "Aunt stored these in the sand for us. But you have brought everyone safely home, so you deserve a precious treat."

All three girls giggled as P'ing flopped his ears and flared his nostrils with curiosity. Quickly Uncle freed him from the harness, and like a trusting young colt, the old mule nosed the food in Sister's hand all the way into the garden. Uncle and Kwei Er walked at his side. At the right moment Uncle called the girls out and locked a surprised P'ing Tan on the other side of the garden wall.

"I cannot believe it," Uncle said proudly as he led them back to the courtyard. "All the Wong children are turning into excellent muleteers!"

Kwei Er heard Mother's laugh added to the others. When he ran to her at the doorway of his house, she squeezed him to herself. The sudden exchange of emotions embarrassed him, and he pulled himself away as soon as Yao's son and wife came up to greet him.

To turn attention away from himself, Kwei Er spoke to the older boy. "I see you have fixed Mother's loom. I am grateful to you for that."

"He also mended the largest of the holes in Uncle's garden wall while you were gone," Yao's mother added.

The older boy smiled. "It is only out of thankfulness to you and your Uncle that I did these things. You saved my father. I will not forget that, ever."

Kwei Er nodded. "Uncle saw your father today. The doctors are pleased with how quickly he heals. In seven days, Uncle will take us all back to Siaochang for church. When we come home that afternoon, your father will be with us."

"I will go to church, too!" Yao's wife announced firmly. "Today, your aunt explained to me why the poster of the bleeding God hangs on her wall. Because of her words, I asked Jesus Christ to clean out my life so that he can live inside me."

"And you, too?" Kwei Er asked Yao's son.

The other boy looked shocked as he shook his head. "Not me! Don't you remember? Your uncle promised we would not have to change our beliefs just because Father is in a missionary hospital." He coldly stepped away.

Mother took Kwei Er's arm. "Come inside. I have some cabbage to cook and I will boil water for you to drink. The meal cannot be special, Son, but there will be a celebration in our house tonight—just because you are safely home."

Kwei Er sat down at his own rough table. His mother carried a basin of warm water to him. He washed the dust from his cold hands and face. When she brought the cabbage and the boiled water, he ate and drank while he marveled at the wonderful sight of seeing Mother tuck all his sisters into bed.

Soon the time came for Kwei Er to sleep. He lay down on his own cot. This night he left the curtain around his bed undrawn, so that nothing would separate him from the feeling of being home. Though he was weary, he could not sleep. More than once, he slipped out of bed to put his knees to the clay floor. He prayed, and prayed again, as though his gratefulness to God would never end.

Finally Kwei Er slipped on his shoes. Feeling his way, he went outside. A light flickered in Uncle's window. Kwei Er waited for a while, then tiptoed to the open doorway to peek inside. He caught his own gasp of surprise, the moment before it sounded on the air.

Uncle was working at the table with the paper, brush, and ink stick Kwei Er had carried all the way from his home on the Grand Canal. Uncle, the hauler whose rough hands refused to touch a book or writing instrument, now was making wet brush strokes in the weak lamplight. Confused and nervous because of what he saw, Kwei Er drew back. But as he turned, he heard Uncle's voice. "I know you are there, Kwei Er. Come, sit near me."

Silently, Kwei Er joined Uncle in the ring of light. Uncle slipped the brush into Kwei Er's hand. "Write for me," he said without emotion. "Do you know the characters in the sign that hangs above the Siaochang gate?"

Kwei Er nodded, too puzzled to speak. His hand trembling, he touched his brush to the ink and made his strokes upon the thin rice paper.

"Now say each character for me," Uncle said, eagerly hunching over the glossy ink marks.

When Kwei Er had done this, Uncle leaned back and sighed. "I want to learn how to read the sacred scriptures, Kwei Er. How many characters must I memorize to do this?"

Kwei Er shrugged tensely. "I do not know exactly, Uncle. Perhaps two thousand?"

"Can you teach me?" Uncle said, his hands flat upon the table.

"I-I could try."

Uncle smiled at him. "You are a fine boy. Sometimes I forget you are not my own son."

He pushed himself from his seat and walked to the doorway. He paused, looking out into the night. "This war has done terrible things to us, Kwei Er. Yet, even in our hardships, I see God's hand of mercy. The experiences we have shared with Li Mu Shi these past two days have caused me to look inside myself. I have been wrong not to listen to Mu Shi's advice. Times are getting harder for our pastor. I must learn how to read."

Kwei Er felt his throat swell with fear as he put down the brush. "Is he going away? Is that why you suddenly wish to read?"

Uncle came back to the table. He sat down. "Only God knows how long Mu Shi will be here. His delay in returning to Siaochang this afternoon was caused by a Japanese officer who caught him on the road. Mu Shi was sent two hours out of his way to be questioned by enemy authorities, and then he was released."

Kwei Er looked at his own hands, thinking about Mu Shi's courage and the great tiredness he must be feeling now.

Uncle took up the brush again. "Until tonight, I thought of Li Mu Shi's dedication to God as being something that was just a part of him—like his fantastic running. But now I see that God desires such complete commitment from everyone who calls on his name." He looked at Kwei Er. "If Mu Shi sacrifices the honor of being home in a country that respects him highly, how can I do less than he does for the people of Hopei?" He paused. "That is why I want to learn to read while Mu Shi is here. I am ready to do everything I can to live wholly for Jesus Christ, even if—or when—Li Mu Shi goes away."

The strange mixture of sadness and joy going round and round inside Kwei Er silenced him.

Uncle gave him the brush again. "We have no copy of the scriptures for ourselves," he said. "But if I told you some verses from memory, could you write them?"

"Yes, I will try."

"Then write this one," Uncle said putting down a clean strip of paper. "'For God so loved the world that he gave his one and only Son. . . .'"

Kwei Er formed each character carefully, as though each was a miniature picture in itself. The brush sighed against the paper as he worked. He felt the joy of seeing a precious copy of God's Word flow from his own head and hand. When he had finished he glanced up at the poster of Jesus that hung on the wall above them.

With Kwei Er's help, Uncle read the characters again and again. Finally Uncle rolled the paper into his hand. "Whenever we are alone, I will practice this," he said. "Perhaps even by Sunday, I will be able to surprise Li Mu Shi with a late, but very special, New Year's gift."

In the days that followed, Uncle did just what he promised he would do. From dawn to dark, when they were on the roads, he talked to Kwei Er about the writing hidden in his jacket pocket. In the evenings, when their hauling for the day was done, Uncle would find a solitary place at home or at the inn where they stayed. There, while Kwei Er listened, he would bow over the characters to practice changing the brushstrokes into spoken words.

When Sunday came, Uncle dressed in clean clothes.

As he left the house at daybreak, he tucked the rolled paper into his jacket pocket. Though everyone, including Yao's son and wife, saw him do it, only Kwei Er knew the reason for his action. Since Yao Feng would be coming back to Nan Kung with them, Uncle decided to take P'ing Tan and the cart. As usual Kwei Er's sisters followed them into the garden at the first light of dawn, hoping to see the hen. Uncle let each of them spread a few wheat grains in the dirt to quiet their sorrows about losing the bird.

Today, as all days, the children jabbered among themselves. "I think the seed is gone from yesterday. Do you think it is the wild birds or the rats that eat it . . . or could it be our hen?"

Uncle shook his head at their mild confusion. "After seven days," he whispered to Kwei Er, "you'd think they'd start giving up hope of ever seeing that bird again."

When Uncle led P'ing Tan into the courtyard the three sisters piled into the cart, delighted for the rare treat of a ride to church. Aunt, and Mother, and Yao's wife walked beside them. As soon as they were away from Nan Kung, Uncle led everyone in singing hymns under the blue, springlike sky. Kwei Er noticed that even Yao's wife tried to follow the notes as they went along. But Yao's son kept his lips together all the way to Siaochang.

When they reached the mission station, the children and women hurried into the plain church building to see their friends. Uncle tied P'ing Tan to one of the hospital porch posts, then led Yao's son and Kwei Er into the men's side of the church. The room was crowded with patients who could walk or be pushed inside in wheel-chairs. Kwei Er and Yao's son looked around for Yao Feng, but the salt seller was not there.

"I am leaving to find Father," Yao's son announced. "I have no reason for wanting to be here, except to see him."

Uncle watched him go, then took a seat. The narrow wooden benches filled quickly as the hospital staff and several local peasant families swelled the crowd. The room rang with countless conversations, until Li Mu Shi walked down the center aisle and turned to speak. He winked right at Kwei Er, before reading an opening scripture and calling out the title of the first hymn.

Though few beside Kwei Er could read, the verses to this song were hung on the wall. Even so, Kwei Er closed his eyes, not needing to read the words as the congregation began singing Mu Shi's favorite hymn.

Be still, my soul! The Lord is on thy side.
Bear patiently the cross of grief or pain;
Leave to thy God to order and provide,
In every change He faithful will remain.
Be still, my soul! Thy best, thy heav'n-ly Friend
Through thorny ways leads to a joyful end.
Be still, m——

Suddenly the walls of the room shook with deep explosions. Instantly the church was silent. Breathlessly Kwei Er listened to the crackles of rifles and the tat-tat-tat of machine guns firing somewhere close by, near the walls of Siaochang. The doctor who had helped Yao Feng rose from the bench behind Kwei Er and ran outside. Immediately Uncle and Kwei Er joined the crowd that pressed out through the church door to the court-yard to see what was going on.

The mission gates, which had been barred for safety, trembled with the frantic pounding of peasants outside. Mu Shi, pushing through the worried clusters of people, finally freed himself to run to the gates.

Listening only for a moment to the cries of those outside, he called, "Let them in! Let them in!"

The old gatekeeper was nearly crushed when forty or more peasants and five haulers with mules and carts burst through the opened gates. "The Japanese attack all around us!" they shouted. "We could think of no safe place—but here!"

"Stay until the fighting passes," Mu Shi said to the terrified crowd. He helped the gatekeeper secure the courtyard, then turned again to the people stranded inside the walls. "We are meeting with the One Eternal and True God right now. Anyone who wishes to join us is invited to come into the church."

The people moved aside so that Mu Shi could lead the crowd into the building. Kwei Er and Uncle were just at the church doorway when Kwei Er heard more pounding on the gates. The old gatekeeper cried for help, and again the pastor came outside and hurried to the entrance. Kwei Er and Uncle stayed at his heels, sensing that something was terribly wrong.

"Now the cries are in Japanese!" the gatekeeper said with horror. "Mu Shi, what is happening outside?"

The pastor held his head to the gate. "The man out-side calls words I know! *'Christian! Peace! Mercy!'*"

"Is it a trick?" the gatekeeper gasped.

Mu Shi looked at Uncle and Kwei Er and then at the crowd tensely watching in the courtyard. "Open the gate! Let the man in!"

Screams of horror rose from the crowd as a Japanese soldier stumbled to Mu Shi's feet. He dropped his rifle. A moment later he collapsed in the dirt. Mu Shi called for Uncle to hold back the crowd while he dragged the unconscious soldier in far enough to close the gate. As he did, a small book dropped from the enemy's hand. "He holds a Japanese Bible." Mu Shi raised his head to the people watching. "Perhaps he is a Christian. That would explain why he dared to come here."

"You can't take in Japanese soldiers!" someone in the crowd cried out. "Whose side are you on?"

Li Mu Shi stayed quiet. A Western doctor Kwei Er had never seen made his way to the injured man, who now lay in a pool of blood. "Someone help me move him," the doctor pleaded. "He's been shot in the chest. We must stop this bleeding, or he will die."

No one except a sun-browned carter moved. "It is too slow to watch the enemy drown in his own blood." The man raised his mulewhip. "I will end life for him at once!"

Mu Shi stepped between the unconscious soldier and the angry carter, while the doctor took off his own shirt to bind the wounded man's chest. "Don't come closer," the pastor warned. "You are on God's property. We do not take life from any man here."

"You are a traitor to China!" the carter seethed.

"The man came here trusting us for help," Mu Shi reasoned. "God's law of love tells me that we must help him."

The crowd was still. Mu Shi stood firm until the foreign doctor Kwei Er knew came to help the one already on his knees beside the injured man. Together they rushed the Japanese soldier in through the hospital door.

"We have had enough of your Western wisdom," the carter said, raising his mulewhip higher as though he considered doing Mu Shi harm.

Uncle suddenly pushed his way to the pastor's side. "If you don't want to listen to a foreigner tell you that there is a time to show mercy even to your enemies, then listen to me."

The other carter stepped back with surprise. "Ma Chuang Fu!" he said lowering his whip. "Let's not bring shame to each other's face. My argument is with the foreign devil, not with you."

Uncle looked at Mu Shi. "I want your Bible," he said steadily.

The pastor questioned him with silent eyes. "I left it in the church. Why do you need it?"

But Uncle was already looking for Kwei Er in the crowd. "Get Mu Shi's sacred scriptures," he said. "Bring the book to me. It is time that those here know that I believe exactly what Li Mu Shi believes."

Not one person moved while Uncle stood waiting for Kwei Er to run to the church. Forcing himself to go, Kwei Er squeezed through the crowd with his heart beating against his chest. Inside the empty building, he found the Bible. Racing back, he put the book into Uncle's hand.

"Turn to the verses I know," Uncle said while all eyes were on them.

"What is this?" the carter across from them huffed.

"You are trying to make us think that you are a scholar now by showing us that you can read?"

"No." Uncle stared directly at him. "I am trying to show you that what I am about to say is not like the stories I create in my mind or draw out from my memory. What I am about to say comes directly from the sacred scriptures. These words have been written by the One True God for me and for you."

With a trembling finger, Kwei Er pointed out for Uncle the first characters of the scripture he could recognize. Uncle put his own finger beside Kwei Er's, and slowly he began to read out loud. " 'God so loved the world that he gave his one and only Son, that *whoever* believes in him shall not perish but have eternal life. God did not send his Son into the world to condemn the world, but to save the world through him.' "

Uncle closed the book. He looked first at Mu Shi, then at the church people, then at the carter who glared at him. "This is the law of love that Li Mu Shi speaks of. The sacred Word does not say that God sent his one and only Son just to the Chinese, or even to the Westerners and the Chinese. It clearly says that *whoever* believes in Jesus Christ will be accepted by God for eternal life."

Uncle looked down at the puddle of blood still at the center of the crowd. "I believe the Japanese soldier who came to this hospital hoped to find mercy by turning to those who love Jesus Christ. That is why Li Mu Shi was right in not turning him away. We, too, need mercy—God's mercy—to save us from the wrong within ourselves." Many from the church began to nod in agreement. But all the carters in the crowd joined the dark-faced one, who turned and walked away when Uncle had spoken his last word.

Li Mu Shi squeezed his fists together as the crowd dispersed. "You can read, Ma Chuang Fu! You can preach, just as I have been praying you would do!"

Uncle frowned. "Perhaps it helped to get the enemy soldier into your hospital," he said glumly. "But other than that, Mu Shi, what good did this speaking and this reading do? The carters I must work with did not believe my testimony. Truly, I did nothing except drive all these men farther away from God."

Kwei Er gulped as Uncle left them. "Maybe this was all my fault. I agreed to teach him how to read those verses."

Mu Shi shook his head. "Don't judge the situation by what you see just now," he advised. "'The Word of God is living and active and sharper than a two-edged sword,' and like the doctor's knife, it must hurt sometimes, before it heals."

8

HAPPY
NEW YEAR

Instead of following Mu Shi back into church, Kwei Er walked to P'ing Tan who dozed by the porch in the warm morning sun. Feeling distant from Uncle, and not wanting the company of anyone else, he stood there thinking about the things that had just taken place. He could understand the carter's anger. The sight of the Japanese soldier had stirred up bitterness in his own throat.

Suddenly a young Chinese man, dressed in the clothes of a hospital worker, bolted from the doorway. He leaped from the edge of the porch and raced to the church. Kwei Er went after him, curious to see why the man ran. The shoulder-to-shoulder crowd inside the church building made it impossible for the worker to squeeze inside. He paced for a moment, while the final words of a hymn died away. Then he shouted through the doorway. "Mu Shi! There's an uprising of patients in the west ward!"

Instantly Kwei Er saw Mu Shi elbowing his way out of church. Uncle soon found Kwei Er and grabbed his arm. With many others, they pushed inside the hospital hallway, expecting to see an angry crowd. But instead, they saw some of the men talking heatedly, though all of them were sitting on their hospital beds. Seeing that there was no cause for alarm, those around Kwei Er and Uncle drifted back into the courtyard. But Uncle and Kwei Er stayed because the man Li Mu Shi was talking with was Yao Feng.

Quietly Kwei Er followed Uncle into the ward, a wide bright room with at least twenty beds. Uncle went to Yao's bedside. "What is happening?" he asked when Mu Shi walked away.

Yao Feng looked at his son who stood behind the bed. "We heard everything that was said in the courtyard just now through the open window. I was angry and decided to do what Mu Shi would not let the carter do. Ten or so men in the room rose up to join in forcing the doctors to hand the Japanese soldier over to us." He paused to look across the ward. "But that man stopped us."

Yao pointed a finger to a man now stretched out wearily on his bed. "He told us that except for Li Mu Shi's law of love, which he applied to the Japanese soldier this morning, we also would be dead."

As Yao Feng spoke, Mu Shi grasped the hand of the man in bed. The patient slowly sat up. Kwei Er realized that the man was Xin Shen, the artist they had rescued with their cart. The dark rags around his neck had been replaced with neat gauze bandages. For the first time, Kwei Er saw parts of Xin Shen's gray moustache and tapered beard.

"You are to be thanked for saving another's life,"

Mu Shi told Xin Shen gratefully.

But the older man shook his head. "I could kill that Japanese man myself!" he struggled, his mouth still stiff because of the wounds on his face. "But you could not, because you follow the God who has the law of love. I did not speak for the enemy's sake, or the sake of these men here, but for you."

Mu Shi eyed him without response.

The man blinked as though overcome by extreme fatigue. "I dedicated my life to the pursuit of wisdom and goodness. But what I saw in forty years was violence, bloodshed, greed. As I lay dying behind my own house, I said to myself, 'The hope of finding wisdom and goodness is dead.' But Li Mu Shi, then you came. And because of *your* wisdom and goodness I have hope again."

Mu Shi's eyes began to smile. "Whatever good you see in me is God in me. I hope you know that."

Xin Shen's eyes warmed too. "I want to know that, if such a thing can be true."

Mu Shi motioned for Uncle to bring the Bible that was still in his hands. He gave it to Xin Shen. "This is the full testimony of God's reaching down to save and love the world," the pastor said. "These words will show why it is possible for anyone to have hope in the goodness and wisdom of God."

Xin Shen looked at the book in his hand. "I will read it," he promised with a sigh. "But right now I will rest."

Kwei Er looked for Uncle as Mu Shi helped Xin Shen stretch out on his bed. He saw that Uncle, Yao

Feng, and Yao's son were missing from the room. Eventually he found the three of them sitting on the porch in the sunlight.

"Every day people came to my bedside to speak to me of Jesus Christ," Yao Feng was saying. "Some of them were Western doctors or nurses. But many of them were Chinese workers."

Uncle frowned as Kwei Er crouched down close to them. "I ask your forgiveness for this," Uncle said. "I did not know that it would be so here."

Yao Feng looked Uncle in the eye. "Why didn't you tell me about such a faith? Why did you keep silent about a living God when you saw me honoring idols and images year upon year?"

Uncle seemed surprised. "You are a friend. I did not want to offend you by making you think that I demanded you to believe as I believed."

Yao Feng shook his head. "I saw the same goodness in you that Xin Shen spoke of seeing in Li Mu Shi. And yet, you never gave a reason why it should be in you, but not in me. So I believed what I had to believe because of your silence. I guessed you were a better, more virtuous man than I could ever hope to be."

"Oh, it's not true!" Uncle protested. "I am the least of men. That is why I did not want to read or speak in public. I did not want anyone to be able to say that I was acting out of selfish pride."

Yao Feng smiled a little. "I believe you, Ma Chuang Fu. And because we are such close friends, I will tell you now that what you hoped would be humility turned out to look like pride. How I wish you had told me everything you knew about Jesus Christ many years ago."

Uncle lowered his head. "How I wish I had, too."

Yao showed his healing arms to his son, to Kwei Er, and to Uncle. "I remember what you said the night you rescued me. You said we would not speak anymore about beliefs until I was well. Now, look, these scars are healing—because you brought me here."

Uncle nodded with satisfaction. "It is God's goodness to both of us."

Yao stood. "When the bandits trapped me I was preparing to burn gifts to the household gods," he said. "Now I am ready to go home to burn my idols for the One True God."

Kwei Er and Uncle stood with Yao and his son. There was no hiding the joy in Uncle's eyes.

"I want Li Mu Shi to be the pastor of my family, too," Yao Feng said. "I am going to ask him now if he will come to Nan Kung to celebrate a belated, but best, New Year's Day with us."

Five days later the sun rose warm and bright on the morning of Yao Feng's planned New Year's celebration. Kwei Er was up at dawn to feed and care for P'ing Tan. As he dropped the mule's breakfast at his feet, he spoke. "Enjoy your well-earned rest today, my friend. It is our first day without work since the start of the new year." Then locking the garden gate, Kwei Er hurried back to his house.

His sisters' faces were already scrubbed clean and their hair was fixed in neat new pigtails. Kwei Er went to wash his own face and hands. As he dried his eyes with the soft cotton towel, Mother came to him with a smile. From behind her back she pulled out a new quilted jacket and a pair of trousers made of her own cloth. "Happy late New Year, Kwei Er!" she said with delight.

"No one else in our family got new clothes!" Kwei Er protested in amazement. "Why did you do such a costly thing for me?"

Mother's eyes blinked away tears. "Because you are the only one who grows day and night without stopping," she teased. "Even your sisters say I was right to find some way to cover those wrists and ankles sticking out from your old clothes."

Immediately Kwei Er drew the curtain around his bed and dressed in the warm new outfit. When he walked out into the courtyard, Aunt and Uncle were there to admire his mother's work.

"Let's be on our way to Yao Feng's house for the celebration," Uncle said, tucking a large rolled piece of paper under his arm. Not one other word was needed to make the little girls run out from the courtyard. Soon they were laughing and giggling outside the salt seller's gate.

They entered to find Li Mu Shi already there. The white ashes of a fire lay in the middle of the courtyard near Yao Feng's feet. "I could not wait one moment more," he explained. "I burned everything at dawn today, even before Mu Shi arrived."

"We wanted something special for today," Second Younger Sister pouted. "But you have already made the special fire Uncle told us we would see."

Her turned-down frown captured Li Mu Shi's attention. "Don't be sad," the pastor said kneeling down to see her eye to eye. "It *is* a very special day when someone turns to God as Lao Yao has done this day. To celebrate, a fine artist back at Siaochang has worked very hard to make a treat for you and your sisters."

Like eager puppies, the girls followed Mu Shi to see what was hidden in the corner of the courtyard under his coat. Their eyes reflected their pastor's own joy as he handed each girl a brightly colored paper fish tied to a stick.

"It really breaths!" First Younger Sister exclaimed as she drew the hollow fish over her head to fill its mouth with air.

"We can do it, too!" Second Younger Sister boasted as even their littlest sister began to run around fattening her paper fish on the morning breezes.

Li Mu Shi pulled on his coat as he watched them. His face was still merry with laughter when he turned to Kwei Er. "And for you, I have also brought a gift."

Yao Feng and Uncle grinned as if they already knew what caused the bulge in Li Mu Shi's pocket.

"This is for you." Mu Shi pressed a Bible into Kwei Er's hand. "Read it daily, my young friend, to yourself and to your family."

"I will!" Instantly uncomfortable with his show of eagerness, Kwei Er glanced at Uncle. "If I have your permission," he added with concern.

Uncle nodded and smiled. "It is a good thing you want to do. You will read the scriptures aloud for us every day while we still have the freedom to do this in our home."

His heart was thrilled by the book in his hand, but Kwei Er's mouth turned down. "Even now, even here, thoughts of our enemies cause us trouble," he said bitterly.

The pastor put a hand on his shoulder. " 'Who shall separate us from the love of Christ?' " Mu Shi waited until Kwei Er smiled again. " 'Shall trouble or hardship or persecution or famine or nakedness or danger or sword . . .?' "

Kwei Er shook his head, remembering that these were scripture verses Uncle had already taught him. "No, Mu Shi. 'In all these things we are more than conquerors through him who loved us. For I am convinced that neither death nor life, neither angels nor demons, enither the present nor the future, nor any powers, neither height nor depth, nor anything else in all creation, will be able to separate us from the love of God that is in Christ Jesus our Lord.' "

Uncle's mouth opened wide. "You know the scriptures in the book of Romans by heart! Truly your memory is growing."

Kwei Er felt his chest expand. "Yes, Uncle, and as we read together I will learn even more."

Uncle hid his emotions by fumbling for the paper still rolled under his arm. He looked at Yao Feng. "Friend, I have little to share with you on this belated New Year's Day. But this one thing has been precious to me and that's why I now give it to you as you begin walking with Jesus Christ." The salt seller took the scroll from Uncle's hands.

"Your picture of God on the cross," Yao said excitedly as he unrolled the paper. "For twenty years I saw this and did not understand. Come, now it will hang in my house in the bare space where my shelf of idols used to be."

Everyone, except the three young children, went in

with Yao Feng. Carefully the man hung the poster above the table pushed against the back wall in the center of the room. Mu Shi finally dared to break the silence by suggesting that they pray.

Afterward, Uncle raised his face to the picture as though he were seeing it for the first time. "God provides everything that is necessary for life and godliness," Mu Shi said to Uncle. "It seems that he already knew what gift was on your heart for Yao Feng. Perhaps that is why this new wallhanging was being made for you."

Slowly Uncle unrolled the paper Mu Shi had put into his hand. A beautiful painting of a peony came into view. "Kwei Er, read what is written with the flower," Uncle said anxiously.

Kwei Er looked around, realizing that for the first time Uncle was not ashamed of the fact that he could read. "The peony holds herself high . . . not to boast of her own beauty, but of the skill of the One who made her." Kwei Er's eyes caught sight of the signature on the left edge of the painting. "It is signed, with gratefulness, by the artist Xin Shen!"

The man is a Christian now?" Uncle asked Mu Shi excitedly.

"Yes," Mu Shi replied. "We have had many talks this week, and now he too believes.

Suddenly the three girls burst in. "Uncle! Uncle! Come quick! There's awful braying in Nan Kung, and we think it must be P'ing Tan's voice!"

Everyone rushed outside.

"That is P'ing Tan!" Uncle shouted after listening a moment for the direction of the mule sounds.

Kwei Er's eyes swelled with fear, but Yao's son

grabbed his wrist and pulled him to himself. "I left one hole unfixed in your uncle's wall!" the boy whispered excitedly. "Every day since I heard of Jesus, I have been asking him to send my hen home if he really is God."

"It's the chicken! Perhaps it's the chicken!" Kwei Er began calling out wildly as he chased Uncle and Mu Shi to their own gate.

But when they got to the garden, they could see nothing but P'ing Tan cowering in the corner, kicking up his heels.

"What is wrong with you!" Uncle scolded with impatience. At the same time Yao's son was squeezing Kwei Er's second youngest sister through the small hole in the garden wall. Everyone—even P'ing Tan—watched nervously, until the little girl emerged again. "Our hen is at the end of the wall in the weeds," Sister squealed. "And she has a nest—with this many eggs!" Proudly she showed all the fingers of her left hand.

"Happy New Year! Happy New Year!" Yao's son shouted, too pleased and shocked to even smile.

Suddenly Kwei Er's littlest sister broke away from Mother. She, too, ducked through the break in the wall to see the hen for herself. A moment later there was a frightful cackle. The hen, followed by the little girl, raced into the garden. The sight was too much for P'ing Tan. His feet flew in all directions. Before Uncle could grab him, he raced through the open garden gate.

Uncle watched Mu Shi run to look out after him. "Chuang Fu!" the pastor shouted. "Your mule has escaped as far as the streets!"

The widest of toothless grins broke across Uncle's face. "You have taught us many things that we can do to be like you, Mu Shi. But, God knows, there is no one else like you! You can do something that we cannot do. Will you do that for us now?"

Li Mu Shi caught the twinkle in Uncle's eye.

"You want me to chase P'ing Tan through the streets of Nan Kung?"

"Oh, yes!" Second Younger Sister shouted.

"Uncle says there are many stories about your running, Mu Shi! But he would never tell us even one!" First Younger Sister added.

"What a happy New Year it would be to see you race against P'ing Tan," Uncle said, speaking for all of them.

"All right, I'll go!" Li Mu Shi said with a laugh. Everyone joined him at the courtyard gate. Then preparing for the run, Li Mu Shi took off his coat and laid it across Uncle's arms.

HISTORICAL NOTE

Chariots to China is based on a true rescue Pastor Eric Liddell and an unnamed Chinese carter made in February 1939. Though Eric experienced most of the incidents woven into this story during his years as a London Missionary Society worker, the names and places used in *Chariot to China* do not necessarily represent real people or locations.

During Eric's time, news of his courageous journey to Pei Lin Tyu spread throughout Great Britain's churches. A print of a peony, painted by the artist who had been rescued, often accompanied the telling of this exciting story about how God was using Scotland's best-loved athlete in far-off China.

Eric Liddell was born of missionary parents in China in 1902. He spent his school years in Scotland, his parents' homeland. His outstanding abilities as a rugby player and a runner came to light when he was at Edinburgh University. Though he avoided much of the publicity that went with being Scotland's most successful athlete, Eric did agree to speak at a Christian rally in 1923. From that point on, his appearances at evangelistic meetings drew many crowds.

When Eric headed for the 1924 Olympic games in Paris, his entire family was in China. The British athletic authorities knew he would not run on Sundays. Eric faced harsh criticism from many sources for his refusal to compete in the Sunday 100-meter trials—until a few days later when he won the 400-meter event in a world-record time of 47.6 seconds! Years later Eric told his wife that he might never have become a great quarter-miler if his convictions at the Olympics had not forced him to run the longer race.

During a combination graduation and Olympics victory celebration at Edinburgh University, Eric quietly announced he was going to China. More than 12,000 spectators turned out for his last Scottish races and hundreds followed him to the train station when he left for Tientsin in 1925.

In 1934 Eric married Florence McKenzie, the daughter of missionaries from Canada. The Liddells' first two daughters were born while he was teaching and organizing athletic events at Tientsin Anglo-Chinese College. At the end of 1937 Eric left his family to take up rural work in Siaochang, the mission station that had been his boyhood home. His older brother Robert was a doctor in the hospital there.

Pressure from the Japanese, coupled with drought and bandit raids, created extreme hardships for the local peasants. Eric walked and biked throughout the region to share God's Word. He stayed in crowded homes, went without food, and risked the same dangers the farmers faced. The Chinese Christians loved him for his unfading smile, his humor, his confidence in God, and his tireless work. Though the Siaochang hospital treated patients of all nationalities, the Japanese eventually destroyed the mission station.

The courage shown by Chinese Christians throughout the nation during this difficult time laid a strong foundation for a church that was to face many more hardships under communist rule.

In 1941 Eric sent his family to Canada, where his third daughter was born. He stayed in Tientsin, working even after the churches were closed by meeting informally with people in their homes. Two years later, following a short-lived hope of being able to leave China, Eric was one of many Westerners forced by the Japanese to go to Weihsien internment center in Shantung Province.

His faith and energy, which had encouraged the Chinese, now ministered to many of the 1800 prisoners who were confined in a concentration camp without adequate sanitation, food, or living space. To the children who were stranded for years without their parents, the former Olympic runner became their own beloved "Uncle Eric." He organized activities, served as a teacher and a guardian for youth, and fulfilled the role of a pastor until a brain tumor claimed his life in February 1945.

The prisoners at Weihsien who attended his funeral represented the thousands worldwide who were shocked and saddened when they eventually learned of the great man's death. His life of humility and faithfulness continues to inspire others through the award-winning film *Chariots of Fire*, the various testimonies and biographies written about him, and his own book *The Disciplines of the Christian Life*.